# LORELEI:

# OFF THE CHAIN

## A CAUTIONARY TALE

§

## TRACI MORRIS

The Java Tree Press *paperback edition:*

Copyright © 2019 Traci Morris

All rights reserved.

Published by The Java Tree Press

Olympia Fields, IL 60461

Printed in the United States

ISBN-13: 978-0692475119
ISBN-10: 0692475117

*Book design by Traci Morris*

# DEDICATION

To my Godmother, Sylvia.

One of the most beautiful people I've ever met, inside and out. Thank you, Auntie, for all of the help, kind words and encouragement you've given me, ALL of my life. It means so much to me. I love you.

## ACKNOWLEDGMENTS

To all of my family and friends who supported me, I am
eternally grateful. To Mom and Cousin Shani, thank you for
providing great inspiration for this story. ;)
And to God, Be the Glory, Forever and Ever...

# PROLOGUE

Lorelei sat on the edge of the Jacuzzi in her posh bathroom with a cigarette dangling from one hand and a bottle of scotch clawed in the other.

*How did I let this happen to me, Lorelei Sampson?*

Just hours earlier, she was humiliated in front of hundreds of Chicago's most elite when her engagement announcement to Andrew Jansen was abruptly cut short by the shocking display of a sex tape of her with some guy. Not taking too much time to think, she ran out of the ballroom where her driver, Gino, was waiting to usher her into the car. It was as if he'd known what was going to happen.

*That was strange. I'll have to think on that later…*

Inhaling smoke hard, she coughed violently as it went down a wrong pipe. The wracking coughs were deeper and raspier than usual. She took a chug of the scotch and mistakenly thought it would soothe her throat. Instead it burned and exacerbated the pain. Choking and coughing in agony, she dropped the bottle to the floor where thankfully, it was too solid to crack. The alcohol spilled out as she fell to the floor on her side, gasping for breath. The scotch began to soak her hair as she fought to breathe. She wondered if this was it. For the first time in a long time, Lorelei felt the fragility of her life. She felt helpless - a foreign emotion. She starts to fade…

*Urban Dictionary: Off The Chain: Wild, raucous, or out of control. Originated from the onset of a dogfight, when dogs are let off the chain and the event begins.*

# UNLEASHED

## PART I

### CHAPTER ONE

*Brooklyn, New York 1992*

Little Lorie Sampson was in fourth grade and hating every minute of it. On her way to school, she unhappily recalled the conversation with her mother, Mallory that morning.

"Mommy..."

"Don't call me that. It's Mother."

"But all of the kids call their mothers, *Mom*."

"Are you other kids?" Her mother gave her a glare that went straight to her soul. No matter what she did, she could not get this woman to show her any affection.

"No, Mother."

Edward and Mallory Sampson were a dynamic duo in every way. Several years ago, they started with a small home appliance store in Queens and expanded their business into a manufacturing juggernaut with an ingenuity that was making investors take notice. Along with appliances, they were now manufacturing phones, TVs, DVD players, cameras and computers. Ed had the big vision and his wife shared his enthusiasm by bringing her business management degree into play. Ed wasn't educated like Mallory, but he made up for it with drive and hard work. He dutifully followed his domineering wife's lead, and although slightly more affectionate towards Lorie than

1

Mallory, it was clear who was running the Sampson family. If Mallory indicated that they had no time to waste on family bonding, then that's the way it went. Together, they were an unstoppable force to be reckoned with. Not even imagining how they took time out to conceive Lorelei, her parents were always busy and never home. This morning was a rare moment where her mother wasn't already at the office with her father.

"Good, now hurry up and go to school and do well so you can be a part of this company. Nothing else is more important than making this money. There will be time later for all of that other bullshit."

"Yes, Mother."

Mallory turned her pinched face down towards the Wall Street Journal that was in front of her. As Lorie put on her coat, she observed Mallory on the sly, careful not to get caught. Her mother was short with drab brown hair that was always pulled back into a weak, wispy ponytail. Along with her gaunt face that was always devoid of makeup, the rest of her had the audacity to be portly.

*Geez, I hope I don't turn out like that.*

Already noting similar physical traits in herself, Lorie made a vow to be gorgeous and wear lots of makeup where her mother didn't. She decided when she was old enough, she would lighten her hair. After all, according to her favorite syndicated eighties shows, it was obvious that blondes had more fun. And she wouldn't get fat either. Unfortunately, she knew the short gene was in full effect because her dad, although much better looking than her mother, wasn't tall either. At ten, Lorie was often mistaken for a first grader in school. When it came to height, she looked more like six or seven. *I'll do what I can with what I've got*, she vowed.

She arrived at the school playground early. With her head down, she made her way towards her favorite swing to eat her regular breakfast of a cold pop tart. Failing to notice that someone was behind her as she sat down, the swing was swiftly removed out from under her. Her school uniform skirt flew up as her pantied bottom met with hard, sharp gravel underneath. She winced in surprise and pain. The laughter throughout the playground was deafening. Looking up behind her, she spotted Jennifer Waldridge, another fourth grader in her class along with her constant accomplice, Ashley Moore. Undoubtedly the culprit, Lorie hurriedly got up to smack Jennifer. But blonde, tall, Jennifer was too fast for Lorie's short steps.

"Why did you do that?"

They laughed as Jennifer played keep away from Lorie's short arms.

"Because I can, you little twit." They giggled and ran off. Humiliated and close to tears, Lorie dusted off her backside and stared angrily at her soiled pop tart. *That's okay, if I eat too much sugar, I'll end up like Mallory's fat ass.*

The bell rang and she made her way towards the school entrance. She felt several dark eyes on her. As she looked to her left, she saw two girls and a guy she knew were in seventh grade, boldly smoking cigarettes. One of the girls had black spiked hair, several earrings and heavy mascara.

She motioned to Lorie. "Come here, kid."

3

TRACI MORRIS

Lorie's eyebrows shot up in surprise as she realized she meant her.

"Yeah, you."

Lorie came to stand in front of the girl who artfully flicked her cigarette in distaste.

"Hey, how you gonna let that lanky, overgrown bitch punk you like that?"

Lorie shrugged. "I don't know. I guess since she's bigger than me, she thinks she can?"

The girl spat something nasty on the ground. "So what. You don't always have to fight back with your fists. There are other ways. See me at lunch. I'll show you how to take care of her and other heifers that come at you incorrect."

Her two companions nodded and laughed along.

Lorelei nodded in agreement. Fed up, she decided she couldn't let Jennifer get away with humiliating her like she had done this morning.

"What's your name, Shorty?"

Lorie winced at the moniker but answered obediently. "Lorie."

She smacked Lorie's hand in a masculine greeting she'd seen guys do.

"Hey Lorie, what's up? I'm Dawn, that's Lucy and Spider." The others, similarly adorned with rings, spiked hair and tattoos, nodded nonchalantly in return.

"Don't forget, right here at lunch."

"Alright, I'll be here."

§

On her hard wooden desk chair, Lorie squirmed all through the morning. She was feeling the pain and pinch from falling on the gravel on her mostly bare behind. She knew there were scrapes and it even felt like there was blood. This only served to anger her more. How dare Jennifer think she could just punk her like that?

Although she was small, there was never any love lost to anyone in school. Due to the cold, atmospheric tension in her household, she was used to cruelty and knew how to cope. She knew she didn't come across as a wimp and wasn't afraid of anyone - just kept to herself and was quiet. Obviously these wenches mistook that for timidity. She would show them. She would listen to any advice Dawn and her crew gave her.

At lunch, Dawn was waiting for her. Spider and Lucy were smoking near the monkey bars while she was taken aside.

"Okay, Shorty, check this out." Lorie was so eager to learn, she overlooked her new nickname.

Dawn broke a green beer bottle on the hard concrete and picked up the jagged, sharp result, holding it by the neck.

"When this 'b' comes outside, you're going to cut her. Simple as that. Nothing too hard or deep, just enough to let her and the others know you are not one to be f---ed with. Get it? Here."

She handed Lorie the jagged piece and just as it was in her hand, Jennifer and Ashley made their entrance onto the playground.

"There's that bitch, go get her."

Seeing nothing but red and without a second thought, Lorie ran up to Jennifer and slashed her throat.

§

Sitting in the police station, Lorie coolly waited for her parents to arrive. As soon as her mother saw her, she walked up to her and slapped her hard across the face.

"You ignorant, stupid, worthless piece of crap. What the hell did you think you were doing? Are you trying to ruin me and your father? What the hell...?"

Ed tried to calm his wife down.

"Cool it Mal, the other girl is going to be okay. The wound wasn't that deep," he turned to Lorie, "but young lady, you are still in big, big trouble. If they decide to press charges, you're on your way to a juvenile detention center. You have possibly just ruined your life."

Still numb and barely feeling the slap, Lorie vaguely contemplated the fact that she had never seen her father this angry.

Upon hearing the news that she hadn't succeeded in murdering Jennifer, she didn't know if she was relieved or disappointed. She had wanted that heifer dead. On the playground, all she could recall was the loud uproar and screams along with the blood gushing from Jennifer's neck. Jennifer's taunting eyes had quickly morphed into fear and dread. It had been comical to see.

*I bet that bitch or anyone else won't mess with me anymore. As long as there is something around to use as weapon, it doesn't matter how little I am. Thank you, Dawn.*

§

Jennifer Waldridge never pressed charges and confessed to her parents what she had done to Lorelei on the swing - even swearing that Lorie had the scrapes to show for it. Both girls were suspended for one week. When Lorie returned to school amidst high fives from Dawn and crew - and kids who'd never even acknowledged her existence - Dawn told Lorie that she had threatened Jennifer while she was down on the ground, bleeding out.

"I whispered in her ear, 'if you press charges - the next time you get cut - you won't live.'"

Lorie laughed thankfully while Dawn placed an arm around her.

"Nobody will ever mess with you again, Shorty."

And nobody did. Even after Dawn and crew graduated or dropped out, she had satisfactorily garnered the reputation of one not to be trifled with. Lorie was officially off the chain.

§

In high school her reputation followed her. But she couldn't forget her ambition to be a 'girly-girl' even if her actions and abrasive exterior proved otherwise. She was able to pull together a crew to do her dirty work.

Just the year before, she started bleaching her hair relentlessly, no matter how much it got damaged. To avoid gaining weight, Lorelei would starve herself for days at a time and picked up an excessive cigarette habit.

Now that her family was firmly established and wealthy, she had to think of her future. Mallory, as she now referred to her mother (with no complaints, by the way), seemed to approve of Lorie's new look and attitude – not that her or her father were ever around for long. Her parents were so busy amassing their fortune that she was left on her own most of the time. That was okay with Lorie, though. She was now every bit as ambitious as Mallory.

Lorie immersed herself into shows like *Dynasty* and *Dallas*, and copped a style from watching her favorite starlets from the Golden Era of television. They were so classy and dignified. She decided they would be the best authorities on how to be glamorous and wealthy. After all, she had nothing else to go by - her parents certainly didn't know. Mallory even picked up a few pointers from Lorie, because now she went to a salon for a light colored hair rinse. She even tried to lose weight and wear makeup, though not as much as her daughter.

Lorie was so paranoid of being plain that she piled on in every make-up category to the extreme.

# CHAPTER TWO

Lorie gave up her virginity when she was thirteen. By the time she became a Liberty High School sophomore at sixteen, she was known to be a girl who got around, but you'd better not call her a whore or she might have you killed.

Ironically, she didn't like sex that much - it was just okay to her. But from watching her favorite shows, it seemed to be the "in" thing to do. She usually made sure the guy used protection, but if not, she made them pull out – which seemed to be effective so far. She had to admit that afterwards, it was nice to cuddle. Knowing they found her cute and petite at four foot ten, most of the time they couldn't resist. Later was usually when she promptly dumped them. She didn't want them to become too clingy and usually they weren't of the right social status. Those guys could forget it. She had a future to consider.

Lorie went after any guy she found an interest in, whether he had a girlfriend or not. At school, there was a boy named Mike Lawson that she had her eyes on. He seemed genuinely nice and made sure to give her a friendly, sexy smile whenever they saw each other. He was not only handsome, but his wealthy parents owned a lucrative software company in Manhattan. With their similar backgrounds, Lorie thought they would be perfect for each other. Unfortunately, he was going out with Karen Mays, a tall cheerleader that was just the type of chick Lorie hated.

For a few days now, Lorie and crew had been bullying Karen. Still intent on being a girly-girl, she let them handle the physical stuff.

Ever since the playground incident, Lorie had been careful not to fight her own battles since she didn't want to ruin her parent's burgeoning status in Manhattan society. Plus, she was real close to getting into Clark Preparatory, a prestigious private high school where she had moved to the top of the wait list. She couldn't mess up now. That's where the crew came in. She had already acquired the reputation for smuggling a switchblade, though it had never been proven. In reality, she didn't have any type of weapon on her (duh - you couldn't get it past the metal detectors anyway), but was active in spreading the rumor to keep silly chicks in line.

Today, they were in the girl's restroom where Libby, her biggest minion, was holding Karen up by the hair against the wall. The girl was terrified as Lorie addressed her.

"You messin' around with Mike? Leave him alone. He's mine."

Karen's expression turned to one of scorn. "Please. He doesn't want *you*. You could never get him."

Nothing roused Lorie's ire more than being told she couldn't have something. Her face turned a splotchy, beet red.

"What, bitch? I can't get him? Oh, I will get him because from now on, if I see you around him, I going to drag you in here and destroy you."

Libby grabbed Karen's hair even tighter.

Karen screeched but didn't back down right away.

"See, that's your problem. Stop trying to take something that doesn't belong to you. He doesn't want you!"

Lorie was so incensed at her words that she did something out of character - drove her fist into the girl's nose. Blood spurted down Karen's lip as she went down in pain, crying and screeching while holding her nose.

"Aaarggh, I think you broke my nose!"

In shock, Libby let her go and Karen fled out of the restroom. She turned a confused eye on Lorie.

"What happened, girl? You lost it."

Lorie desperately needed a cigarette. Trembling, she pulled one out of her vintage snap pocketbook. She lit it up and started dragging in gulps of smoke before quickly stubbing it out.

"I don't know. She pushed me too far. Let's go."

Once outside the bathroom, rumors were flying that Karen had been taken to the infirmary and consequently had to leave the premises for a hospital. It was that bad. Lorie had really broken her nose.

*Man, I cannot let this get back to my folks.*

Stressed about the possibility, at lunch she went to some guy's house that had been sweating her. She really needed something right now, but couldn't figure out what. When he tried to pressure her for a quick romp, she pushed him away. Her mind was so preoccupied about the incident that she couldn't be bothered any longer. She left and walked back to school smoking a cigarette.

Rumors were still circulating and she received a few knowing glowers, but no one was bold enough to address

11

her. Throughout the day she expected to be summoned to the school office, but for some reason, it never happened.

Facing another evening without her parents, she decided to go to the movies with another guy who had been pressuring her to go out with him. Later, they sat outside her house in his car and made out heavily. They ended up having sex. Afterwards, she let him hold her, but he was musty and she pushed him away. She got out the car and stormed into the house in frustration. There had been a guy from last week who smelled much better than these two today. She filed away the priority to remember who he was and to call him. Right now, she had too much on her mind.

The next day at school, Karen was said to possibly need reconstructive plastic surgery as her nose was crooked and this could ruin her budding modeling career. Although the news made her gleeful, Lorie was still really nervous that it would travel back to her parents. Again, no summons to the office that day.

Alone, she made her way home after school. When she passed the football bleachers, a tall burly guy whom she believed was a senior, blocked her path. He came out of nowhere and as she looked around, there wasn't another soul in sight. Ominously, the sky grew dark and threatened to rain.

"You Lorie?" he asked.

"Yeah, so what?" she answered defiantly while smoking a cigarette.

Unexpectedly, he grabbed her arm and proceeded to drag her under the bleachers.

Resisting, she tried to fight back but he was too strong.

"What are you doing? Let me go, you big gorilla!"

He dragged her under the bleachers and down onto the grass. He was hunched over her, holding her down by the neck. She was unable to move an inch. His eyes were full of rage. For the first time in years, she was really afraid.

"Lorie, you like bullying girls and punching them in the face? Huh? I got something for you, then. Payback." Her eyes bulged in fear and he laughed. "Oh yeah. How does it feel to be on the other side?" She tried to squirm but was deadlocked. "I told her not to report you so I could take care of you. That girl whose nose you broke, Karen? That's my little sister, bitch!"

Horrified, Lorie realized that he was indeed Jeff Mays, Karen's older brother who was a senior and infamous offensive end on the football team. Her blood ran cold. She hadn't thought about him when she was bullying Karen.

*I failed to consider all of the logistics. Damn, I'm slipping...*

By this time, he had his hand over her mouth while tears began to stream out of her eyes. She was in big trouble. He was so huge in contrast to her that he would probably kill her once he started beating her. But... something else was happening. He began ripping her blouse open and lifting up her uniform skirt to get between her legs. Dread washed over her. If he was thinking of doing what she thought he was thinking of doing, she would rather he killed her.

"Oh, I've heard about you. You get around, you little slut. I have plenty of boys that have gotten a piece of this and I might as well see what the fuss is about."

Soon his pants were down and he was on top of her. She was never able to let out a scream while he forcefully

13

violated her. This was so different from her other encounters, she thought. For one, it was excruciating because she wasn't prepared. And he was brutal. His heavy form weighed down on her as he continued his assault while she looked off to her right in a daze. It seemed to go on for an eternity. *This is not happening to me.* He finally grunted to a finish and climbed off of her, readjusting his pants. Once he took his hand away from her mouth, she couldn't utter a word.

"Say something about it, slut, and I'll get you again. As much as you've been around, nobody will believe you crying rape or some sorry crap like that." He turned to walk away but paused. "And just for the record, it wasn't all that. Bitch." He spat towards her, just missing her face by an inch. He stalked off, leaving her debased and painfully exposed under the bleachers. It began to rain.

This was the worst day of Lorie's life.

§

She thought it was the worst day, but it was actually the next one. Jeff had spread the rumor around school that she had let him do it to her under the bleachers. She wasn't as upset about that because she had been subjected to mild rumors before. It was what happened next.

Mike, the guy she had a crush on, approached her.

"Hey, Lorelei."

Her heart was beating fast at him calling her full name and he was smiling. He had such strong, beautiful features.

*Maybe today will be alright after all.* She tried to give a sexy half-smile.

"Hey, Mike."

Then his smile abruptly fell. "I'm really disappointed in you right now, Lorelei. Not only did I hear you beat up Karen - who I was actually considering dumping for you since we seemed to have more in common - but you gave it up to her meathead brother?" He scrunched up his face in disgust.

Her eyes grew voluminous in shame. "Look, Mike, that's not what happened…" she sputtered to explain.

"Look, my family has a reputation to uphold and yours too I would think. They would never let me be with someone who's so violent and trashy like you. I know you like sex and all and that's not a problem, but this was way too much. What you did was foul. You are one mean ho. Peace out."

He walked off and she stood there, stunned. This was not how she saw things playing out…and he called her a *what*?

Now, *this* was the worst day of her life.

After that, Lorie clammed up and became introverted. She no longer hung out with anyone, including Libby, Gino and the crew. She kept to herself and was sick to her stomach most days. Remembering the physical attack by Jeff and the lethal verbal attack from Mike left her cold inside. She abhorred the thought of sex or anything related.

It just so happened that a week and half later, she was accepted to Clark Preparatory Academy. The timing couldn't have been more perfect. Lorelei transferred out of Liberty High School without a backwards glance.

As she got situated on her first day at Clark, she realized there were no metal detectors.

*Check.*

Although she was in orientation all day, she noticed a few shady girls mean mugging her on the low. The next day she was prepared. These Upper East Side chicks were more refined than Liberty girls, but tried to pretend they were more treacherous. *What a joke.* Underneath the designer shoes, expensive makeup, and salon perfected hair was a nasty, delusional undertone. One that she would have to nip in the bud, right away. She got flashbacks from fourth grade of the way they must've perceived her: short, timid and one who could be screwed over. *Not.*

She boldly entered into what was a luxury powder room compared to the restrooms at Liberty High. Once inside, the three tall, shady chicks from yesterday were glaring at her with their arms crossed. *Let's do it.*

After completing her business and exiting the stall, the one that appeared to be the lead chick stepped towards Lorie while she was washing her hands. The other two stood away with a snicker threatening their expertly made up faces.

"Who you be, Shorty?"

*Hell no, she didn't. High society trick sounded so stupid trying to talk ghetto.*

In the blink of an eye, Lorie grabbed lead chick's hair and snatched her towards the wall. Thrown off guard, the girl complied like a ragdoll. Kneeing her up in her crotch to keep her in place, Lorie expertly flipped open the switchblade that was stashed in the side of her tights. She placed it up to the girl's throat and leaned in very close to her ear as she glanced at the other two in warning.

Lead chick's eyes were wide with alarm as Lorie spoke low through gritted teeth.

"Let me tell you something, bitch. I'm from Liberty High in Brooklyn and just because I'm petite - make no mistake - you do not want to f--- with me. Okay? Don't get it twisted. I have been known from fourth grade to slice a bitch's neck. Check me out."

She moved her hand to grip the girl's uniform tie, choking her a bit while the knife in the other hand went a little deeper into the girl's skin. "Answer me, ho. Let me know you understand."

She looked down into Lorie's livid blue eyes, seeing a wickedness that shook her to the core.

She nodded, sputtering, "Yes, I get it. I understand."

"What's your name, trick?"

"A...man...da. Amanda."

Lorie slowly let go of her tie and backed away but kept the knife up to her neck.

Still keeping her voice menacingly low, she motioned to the other two.

"Alright, Amanda, make sure those two sluts understand and every other tramp in this school. Got it?"

"Yeah, I got it."

"By the way, hos, the name is Lorelei Sampson. Don't ever forget it. Hear?"

"Yes," they all answered in unison. Amanda straightened her clothes and all three high-tailed it out of there.

Lorie calmly reapplied her makeup and noted she was getting low on blue eye shadow - she could never have enough. Looking at herself in the mirror, she half-smiled to herself.

*Had to let them know what's up because I don't have time for the dumb stuff anymore. I've got a reputation to build for high society. Like Mallory says, it's all about these dollars.*

# CHAPTER THREE

*The West Household: 1999*

"Derrick, come here. I want you to meet somebody."

He walked through their rickety apartment hallway towards the living room where his mom was sitting on the sofa. Standing no taller than three feet was a chubby, sad looking child with a dried tearstained face that looked up at him with watery eyes. She had brown, curly hair and her blue, almond-shaped eyes seemed to look straight through him.

He couldn't say anything so he just stared. *Who was this child?*

"Derrick, meet your new little sister, Gail." His mother turned to the child who was looking back and forth from him to his mother. "Gail, this is your big brother, Derrick." At that moment, neither moved an inch. After a moment of shock passed, he was able to speak.

"Mom, what?"

"I told you I've always wanted a little girl. So, here she is. Surprise! You know I've been signed up as a foster parent for a while and they brought me an adorable one and a half-year old who is available for adoption. So don't be rude, say hi to Little Gail."

He snapped out of his stunned stupor. After all, his mother had tried to raise him with some manners.

"Hi, Gail," he reached out his hand awkwardly, "pleased to meet you." A little grubby hand reached out to touch his.

"Hi, Daddy."

He stared in shock at her words.

His mother laughed. "I'm sure you're not the first one she's said that to."

But intense blue eyes were staring at him as if no mistake had been made.

§

For the next week, Gail learned his name but also continued to call him Daddy from time to time. He had gotten so used to it he stopped correcting her. In all honesty, it endeared her to him more. The weird thing was that she fit in so well.

When he took her to the corner store, Mrs. Hoffman, who had known them for years, remarked on how much she looked like he and his mother. He had to agree. He had darker hair, but other than her eyes being blue to his brown, they were almond shaped like he and his mom's.

Little Gail didn't say much but he could see the intelligence and curiosity in her eyes. He also noticed something else strange while he was helping her into her pull-ups. She had a moon shaped birthmark low on her left hip that was nearly identical to his in the same spot. *Crazy coincidence*, he thought.

He graduated from high school and got a summer job. The next months flew by and he found himself looking forward to getting home to play with his new little sister every day. Little Gail was starting to talk more and more.

She was a feisty little thing and they play-fought and tumbled often. He was starting to adore the little monster.

One day he got home early and noticed his mom and Gail weren't there yet. As the day wore on into evening, he began to worry. His mom hadn't gotten a cell phone yet and he had no way to contact her. The house phone rang. The person on the other end told him he needed to get down to Breckenridge Hospital right away. There had been an accident.

Once he got to the hospital, he was told his mother and sister had been in a car accident. She had him listed as next of kin. They had been sideswiped and were both in serious condition. After what seemed like ages, he was finally able to see his mother in the intensive care unit. Even while she was hooked up to all sorts of tubes and monitors, her eyes lit up in recognition and relief.

He held back tears at seeing his mom in this condition. She seemed to have casts and bandages everywhere. Her face was swollen and bruised. He willed himself not to cry.

From her expression, he knew she wanted him to take off her oxygen mask so she could speak.

"No, Mom, you need that on."

Her eyes pleaded with him to remove it, so he gently lifted it off.

"Derrick," she squeaked out in a raspy voice. She cleared her throat to speak louder. "Derrick...you need to... take care of your sister."

His heart lurched in panic. She was giving up.

"No, Mom, you're going to take care of her because you're going to get better and get out of here."

She weakly shook her head once.

"Listen to me, baby. Just in case…you need to take care of yourself… and your sister. Listen closely. Underneath the dresser… is a file box. It has… everything you need to know is in there, including… Gail's papers…" She started to drift off. Then she shook her head as if trying to gain mental clarity.

"Ma…?" The tears were now streaming unchecked down his face.

"Listen, son. Just… find the papers. I love you… so much.

He put his head down towards her side.

"I love you too, Mom. Please… don't go."

She looked at him with such love as a lone tear went down the side of her face.

"I love you… and tell Gail…that I love her…"

A machine flat lined.

§

After crying for more than thirty minutes before he was told he had to leave the room because of procedures, he went out into the hallway. Distraught, he almost forgot about Little Gail until a doctor mentioned that he needed to talk to him regarding her. A few rooms down from his mother, he looked in on his little sister who was unconscious and looked so small in the huge bed.

*She is all I have left.*

The doctor told him that she had just come out of surgery where they stitched up a huge laceration on her left thigh. She was in pretty good shape since she had been on the opposite side of impact in the back. However, she had been cut deeply and although stable, she needed a transfusion after losing quite a bit of blood. The hospital was currently waiting for a shipment of a rare blood type, AB negative. He knew that he was the same blood type so he volunteered. Perfect match. While he held in his grief regarding his mother, he numbly thought about the fact that coincidentally, he and Gail shared the same blood type. That, along with the birthmark and other similarities had him curious out of his mind.

§

Later that week, Derrick held a small service at a local funeral home for his mother. Everyone that knew them in their community came out to say farewell to Barbara West. His mother's brother, Uncle Marty, came in from down south and invited him to relocate once he got everything settled. He wasn't sure what his plans were, but he promised to keep that in mind.

Little Gail was still in the hospital and wouldn't be released for a few days. When he went home the day his mother passed, he located the safe box. Inside, his mother had all of the official documents including her own and his birth certificate, etc. On top, there was an insurance policy leaving him $250,000 dollars which was more than enough to take care of the arrangements and he and Little Gail for a while. Underneath, she had the legal adoption papers on Gail that had yet to be finalized and something about previous foster parents. There were forms that his mother filled out for an amended birth certificate with her birth date, his mother's name and Little Gail's new last name-to-be, West. There was a mountain of other documents that he would sift through later.

When he visited Gail the next day, he saw a friend from high school, Troy, who had a part time job as a lab technician at the hospital.

They greeted each other with a somber hand slap.

"Man, I'm real sorry to hear about your mom," Troy said.

"Thanks, man."

"How you holdin' up?"

"I'm okay. Here to see my little sis. She should be out soon. How long you been working here?"

"About five or six months. It's cool. I work in the lab for blood testing."

A light went off in his head.

"Hey man, how much is DNA testing?"

"It ain't that cheap. About two hundred and fifty bones. Why? You got some girl in trouble?" he asked, laughing.

"Naw, nothing like that," then he paused as he thought about it, "at least I don't think so," he laughed out nervously. "I just want to check something out. I need a test. Even though Little Gail was in the process of being adopted by my mom, she looks eerily like me and my mom. Also, we have the same birthmark in the same spot."

"Oh man, that's crazy. You've been dippin.'" Troy gave Derrick a hand slap.

He laughed it off. "Seriously, man, I just want to know if she's related."

"I can do a test right now. I just have to get her blood vials and some blood from you. And the money, of course."

"Cool."

§

A few days later, he was in Gail's hospital room watching *Barney* with her. Although she still had a huge bandage on her leg, she was restless and couldn't wait to get out, which was to be tomorrow. He had explained to her that mommy had gone "Bye-Bye" to Heaven in which Gail responded, "Oh no, she gone?" And then she looked sad. It had shocked him that she had caught on so fast. Some kids were a lot smarter than given credit for. She seemed listless for a day and then oblivious about what had happened. She was still calling him Daddy every now and then. He couldn't deny that her regular use of it only fueled his curiosity more.

When Troy knocked on the open door, his eyes looked like a deer in headlights when he motioned for Derrick to come out. He told Gail he'd be right back and went into the hallway.

"Man, you are not going to believe this. Here."

Troy handed him an official looking document with the results of the blood test.

It told him he could *not* be excluded from being Gail's father. Based on testing results obtained from analyses of fifteen different DNA probes, the probability of paternity was 99.9999 percent.

Gail was his daughter.

§

Shocked beyond belief, he went back into the room in a daze, never taking his eyes off Little Gail. Eventually he was able to sit back down in the seat next to her bed. He looked at her in wonder and then smiled as his eyes began to water.

Ironically, she asked, "Wat wong, Daddy? You okay?"

Her chubby hand came out and inelegantly stroked his cheek, now wet.

He would never correct her name for him again.

He choked out a laugh. "Yes, baby girl. Daddy's going to be okay."

She reached up as far as she could with her injured leg and gave him a big kiss on the cheek. He hugged her back tightly and in that instant, his love for her grew a million-fold. It was then that he knew there had to be a God that brought his orphaned child back to him. He would make sure he wasn't an absentee father like his had been. It couldn't have been a coincidence. And it seemed as if Little Gail knew all along. What were the odds?

"Okay." Then she resumed watching the conclusion of Barney.

He didn't take his eyes off of her for the rest of the day.

After leaving the hospital that night, he was finally able to give serious thought to the situation. He wracked his brain trying to figure out how this had happened. If she was almost two, he knew that Gail had been conceived when he was a sophomore with some girl he had gotten with that gave her up for adoption. That much was clear.

Although he had slept with plenty of chicks by now - back then, it was few and far between. He started whittling down the choices based on Little Gail's looks and her actual birth date which was listed as September 4, 1997. He thought hard about who he had "hooked up" with nine or so months before that. He knew he and a few girls had been stupid enough not to use protection. In order to remember the girls he was after at the time, he had to recall what school activities were happening or the weather. He narrowed it down to four girls. Were any of them showing before summer break? He couldn't remember any girl rumored to be pregnant. Belinda and Marissa had dark complexions, so due to Little Gail's light coloring, he ruled them out. That left Leslie and...*what was her name again*?

# CHAPTER FOUR

*Chicago: 2013*

*I'm still alive…*

Lorelei awakened, feeling a nasty liquid coming from her mouth. Her whole world was tilted sideways. Still on the floor, she tried to sit up but her drenched head seemed stuck to the expensive tile. *Ugh, I vomited and I'm lying in it.*

There was a massive puddle of it under her face and her head was soaked with scotch. Revolted, she used all of her might to force herself up onto her elbows. The bathroom did three-sixties while she hurriedly closed her eyes and held her breath until it stopped. She was jacked up. After a few minutes, she was finally able to turn the shower on. As she carefully climbed in, it was brought back to her remembrance why she was in this condition in the first place. That's right - the engagement party…

*Mistress of Ceremony, Diane Shearer announced, "Thank you for coming out to celebrate this special evening for Andrew Jansen and Lorelei Sampson. The couple would like to give everyone a glimpse of their vision for the future alliance of Jansen Worldwide Capital and Sampson Electronics. Please focus your attention to the screen."*

*The logos for JWC and Sampson appeared on the screen along with five seconds of pompous introductory music. Then it shot to a grainy, dark room with loud moans that began to permeate throughout the ballroom. "Ahh, ahh...oh..." People looked around at each other in question and awkward embarrassment. Lorelei, on the verge of outrage that such a technical malfunction could occur at her party, stood up. Then the camera zoomed in and there was a close-up showing Lorelei's face. She was beneath a muscular man (clearly not Andrew) that was nailing her into the mattress. Her face was contorted and unmistakable.*

*A huge gasp went through the room and all eyes descended on Lorelei. Stunned, she was paralyzed as she realized what she was seeing. It was a sex tape where she was the leading lady. Flash bulbs from the invited media went off like blazes while she stood there like a frightened gazelle. Finally, her faculties kicked into high gear and she flew out the side exit where Gino was waiting with the car door open.*

As she recalled it again, a humiliation that she hadn't felt in years washed over her. Her reputation for being frigid had undergone a colossal shift, going from *The Ice Princess* to *Two-Time Cheating Whore* in less than an hour.

She knew once she located her phone, it would be bombarded with text messages from her parents and associates about her "big screen" debut. Everything that she had tried to avoid and protect in terms of the Sampson reputation had been destroyed in less than an hour. Her head spun. *I can't do this. Somebody, please help me.*

In the shower, she wept as she realized that this punishment must be the culmination of all of the dastardly deeds she had committed in life. This was the ultimate disgrace that usually never went away – just ask your favorite reality stars. She had to figure out why this had happened to her and what she should've done differently...although the truth was pretty clear.

She'd had it coming to her...

In conclusion, there was no use trying to justify her actions. Nothing she had done in the last twenty years had made much sense. When something devastating like this occurred, why was it so clear to see the wrong paths that were taken? Was it because she thought she could continue to get away with it? She had been getting away with so much; she believed herself invincible.

Why would she sleep with a random guy when she was almost to the finish line, amassing a huge global joint empire with Jansen Worldwide?

*Because I didn't think I would get caught.*

She had previously been engaged to James Jansen, oldest son of the Jansen Worldwide Capital fortune. They had been on and off for years since college - until James decided to fall for one of his jump-off chicks. Breaking the promised conglomerate merger between their families, Lorelei was unceremoniously dumped...but not before she'd gotten even. But that's another story...

Still able to seal the deal and with dollar signs in her eyes, she hurriedly got engaged to his younger brother, Andrew.

Andrew had made it clear that he was totally in it for business reasons and was still in love with his old girlfriend, Angela. Instead of fighting like she had done with James and his women, she let it go. She had already run out of energy and couldn't bring herself to really care. Previously, she had convinced herself that she loved James and that he was worth fighting for. But the way she ran blindly towards the new deal, she could see that she never really loved him. She was always in love with the objective: More money.

Although she and James weren't intimate because of her past aversions to sex and his dalliances with other women, she held out for any semblance of affection from him. In their college days they had slept together a few times, but it didn't last. Clearly, she wasn't willing enough for him. Maybe that halted his attraction to her. Come to think of it - was he *ever* really attracted to her?

Last year, when the threat of losing him for good became real, she was willing to hang up her abstinence card and do whatever he wanted. Unfortunately for her, it was too late. Uninterested, he had moved on in every way possible. She continued to hold out hope for him and didn't stray. After all, they were to be married, and unlike him, she was faithful.

In contrast, Andrew was never interesting or attractive to her in any way. He was a kid and felt like a little brother. He had just graduated from school, for goodness sake!

Therefore, completely emotionally unattached, she decided to get back out on the scene. She did something she hadn't done since her college days with James - had sex with a guy. Just like way back in high school, finding someone was easy. Seems there was always someone lined up for that. What she hadn't anticipated was being recorded.

And it had only happened once.

Through her muddled mind, she tried to think back. Remembering how the camera zoomed in, someone else had to be working it...

She was set up.

Weeks ago, she had been introduced to a muscle-head named Jeremy at a society affair after party. He was nice looking enough, but kind of cheesy, though. He had zero personality but would do. He pretended that he was really into her and sweated her constantly, no matter how much she cussed him out. He wouldn't let up and now she knew why. Deciding that there was only one reason for them to be together in the first place - because he certainly wasn't wealthy - she slept with him. Contrary to what the tape portrayed, it wasn't that great, either. But to her, it never really was...

Evidently, he was behind the incident and working with someone else - obviously an enemy of hers. She had quite a few of those so there would be no way to narrow it down. She was too revolted to view the tape again for clues. And she refused to contact that slime bag, Jeremy for an explanation - she wouldn't dignify him with her call. He was probably incognito anyway. With Gino not to be trusted, she had no means of following up.

She just needed to accept that she'd been had. Bitterly, she chuckled at the irony. Knowing that someone would go to these lengths to set her up like that only reinforced what a messy life she led.

She was fed up and tired. She had been so close to the finish line and had failed epically. An ambition that had been over twenty years in the making - gone down the drain.

*I don't know what to do, now.*

She exited the shower, cleaned up the disgusting floor and put on her fluffy terry robe. Looking out of the top floor window of her Gold Coast condo, it was early morning.

Clearly, she was out on the floor like that all night. Shaking her head, she lit up another cigarette and looked at her phone with dread. The light was flashing with messages. After inhaling, she started coughing and hacking again. The sound coming out was a low whooping cough accompanied with massive pain. That was how it felt before she passed out, she remembered between wretches.

*What the hell is wrong with me?*

She quickly stubbed out the cigarette, figuring she wouldn't be doing that for a while. Remembering she was supposed to be fearless, she checked her phone. There were a combined total of thirty two voice and text messages. Most were from Mallory who was incensed and demanding she call back. A few were from some of her fake associates, including Miki. She didn't want to talk to any of them. None of them would be sincere. They would be secretly happy this happened to her.

She had Gino from high school but he didn't count. She'd brought him over from New York because he'd needed a job. That's probably the only reason he was loyal to her. So, no real friends - she didn't have those. Maybe because she wasn't a good friend, either.

None of the calls were from Andrew. While she didn't feel anything for him, it was still sobering to realize that he didn't care one bit that she'd slept around on him. *My life is a complete mess.*

She tapped her mother's number. Mallory picked up on the first ring.

"Still a disgusting tramp, I see. One day you're going to think before opening your damn legs. Haven't you learned anything by now? Where have you been? Do you realize what you've done? Huh? Answer me?"

Lorelei sighed. "Yes, I do."

Her mother seemed to wait for more explanation but Lorelei had nothing more to say. She was done. It was over.

"What? You have nothing more to say? What are you going to do about this? You've just cost us millions. There is no earthly reason why Andrew should marry you now and there is no strong arming his parents into forcing their son to marry a two-timing, cheating slut. It's over for you. Don't you get it? You blew it for us all. I hate you for this!"

Resignedly, Lorelei sighed into the phone.

"I know Mallory. You've always hated me. Probably Ed, too."

Noting the change away from Lorelei's typical confrontational response, her mother grew quiet for a moment.

"That's not true - your father loves you very much."

Lorelei chuckled bitterly under her breath."What about you, *Mom*?"

She heard her mother gasp through the phone. She hadn't attempted to call her that since she was ten and this was a conversation they hadn't had. Mallory's uneasiness came through the line loud and clear. After several stunned moments, she spoke defensively.

"What about me? You're my daughter, aren't you? I've taken care of you all of your life, haven't I? What kind of question is that?"

Lorelei sighed inwardly. She knew she would never get a confession of love from Mallory. Now that she had ruined their deal of a lifetime, those were three words she could forget about. Then she had an epiphany. Was that the ultimate goal she had been striving for all her life? Her mother's love? Deciding to ponder that thought later along with a lot of other things, she changed the subject.

"Mallory, I can't stay here any longer. I know Chicago media is having a field day and I don't know who may be lurking outside this place. Get me out of here."

Thankful the subject was changed, Mallory put on her CEO voice. Problem solving was what she did best.

"Alright, you need to disguise yourself as best as you can. Wear a hat and shades or something. I can have Maurice pick you up in the back and take you to O'Hare. I'll have Myra reserve a ticket for you to fly to our place in Savannah. It's quiet there and nobody will be looking for you. Got it?"

"Ugh, the property in Georgia? Why not one of the islands?"

"Because that's where they'll be expecting you to go. Those are not as excluded and private as Savannah. Now get ready because I don't want to hear it. You made this mess and you're going to do as you're told. Got it?"

All of the fight gone out of her, she responded, "Got it."

# BOUND

## PART II

### CHAPTER FIVE

Once on the plane to Georgia, she relaxed for the first time. Stretched out in First Class, she contemplated her next move. In the nineties, Ed bought a huge house in Savannah where his family originated. Being sentimental, he had the huge mansion constructed only miles away from where he was a kid. Before that, Ed hadn't been back home since they had gotten wealthy in New York. He obviously had fond memories of his upbringing.

He had even named Lorelei after his southern belle grandmother.

Unfortunately, all of his family had either migrated north or passed on. And in her opinion, the new place wasn't that great. She had only been once and didn't like it. There was nothing to the house - it was colossal for no reason. There hadn't been much effort put into the design and it didn't really fit in with the other plantation style homes. It was just… big.

She planned on staying for a few weeks until things died down. She was in contact with some of Sampson's IT professionals about the sex tape video that was now online. She had to keep down the bile when they informed her that it had already gone viral with close to two hundred thousand views. She screeched into the phone for them to remove it, ASAP.

In regards to Gino, her suspicions were confirmed. He knew about the possible leak and was paid to keep his mouth shut. He wouldn't reveal who was really behind it with Jeremy. That was Gino, only loyal to top dollar. Since Gino was her only henchman, there was nobody she could call to get more information out of him. She wasn't Mafioso or anything. And with what Gino had on her, she definitely couldn't involve the police. Amazingly, he hung up after sincerely wishing her the best.

After the two hour flight, she rented an Audi, programmed the address into the GPS and made her way to their estate. She had to admit, Savannah was a beautiful town. With its stately plantations, beautiful azalea gardens and landmark giant oak trees hanging with Spanish moss, it was a sight to behold. It was so different from the big cities she was accustomed to. Feeling a million miles away from all of her worries, she began to feel a calm she hadn't felt in a while.

§

The home wasn't far from the famed historic district. Once inside the stately house, a waft of rank, moldy funk permeated her senses.

*What the hell? When was the last time this place had been tended to?*

She immediately dialed Mallory.

"I'm here. There's a foul odor in here. Don't we have people to tend to this place?"

"What are you talking about? Of course we do. Someone was just there a week ago. Is it not clean?"

Surveying the area, she wiped her finger across the dining room table. It certainly looked clean, so where was this smell coming from?

"Yeah, it seems pretty clean." Sniffing, she continued walking in the direction of where the odor was the strongest. It was near the basement door. Opening it, all she had to do was look down towards the bottom of the stairs to see that it was flooded. "You've got to be kidding me. This place is flooded. That's where the smell is coming from."

This was really not her day.

"Flooded? Ridiculous. Are you sure?"

"I'm looking right down at about two inches of water or so in the basement. I'm not going down there. And I'm not staying here either. It reeks."

"My goodness, no." Mallory went into problem solver mode. "I'll get Myra to locate a local plumber to take care of the problem and a clean-up crew. You're going to have to find someplace else to stay until after cleanup. A hotel or something. Check on your phone."

Sighing in disbelief, Lorelei agreed and hung up. *Incredible.* Back in the car, she searched four star hotels and decided on The Brice Hotel. The boutique hotel was located on Washington Square near the River District. Passing River Street, she couldn't help but admire the view. Admittedly, she was relieved not to have to stay at the house. It stunk and was spookier and uglier than ever.

The modern gray façade and yellow awnings of The Brice were inviting as it hit her how exhausted she was. Once in her comfy suite, she undressed and fell out.

That evening, she woke up realizing she was starving. Dressed in one of her white trademark Chanel dress suits, she made her way out the hotel and down towards some place to eat. She got a few stares from people who were dressed casually in shorts and tees. She was used to it. They were just jealous that she was so glamorous.

Deciding on Olde Pink House, she sat and enjoyed her crab soup, pork shank and a glass of wine.

*Boy, did I need a drink.*

She really needed a cigarette too, but was still traumatized by what happened last time.

She drank one glass, and then another as her mind involuntarily went to the last time she was out in a nice restaurant in Chicago. At that time, she'd taken for granted how good she had it. Now she realized a chapter of her life was over. *What's the use?* She motioned for the waitress to bring her a whole bottle of their finest...

§

"Ma'am, you're going to have to leave. We're closing."

She tried to lift her head towards the server as she gathered her bearings. She had fallen out face flat onto the table.

"Huh?"

"You've been sleep for a while and we're closing."

"Oh," she mumbled, disgusted at her drool that was on the table.

Still disoriented, she paid her bill and tried to get up. After a few feeble attempts, she was able to stagger towards the door. Once outside, she had no idea where she was in relation to the hotel. After stumbling and almost tripping twice, she took off and picked up her four-inch Jimmy Choos and walked a few blocks barefoot. She could see the river coming into view. She thought the hotel was nearby but couldn't be sure. On the boardwalk, there were plenty of people going to and fro and there was a live band playing. She stumbled to a bench.

*Lorelei Sampson, this is a new low even for you,* she said to herself. *What are you doing?*

Through her clouded mind, she could comprehend that this was not a good look. She sat looking over the water as she tried to sober up. Couples strolled arm and arm, some with children, laughing and enjoying life. She had never had anything like a true loving family. After a while, she stopped desiring it. She had been so busy trying to marry into more wealth that a real marriage not connected to dollars wasn't an option she had ever considered. After her disastrous experiences in high school and her failed engagements to the Jansen Brothers, she was forever jaded by the thought of true love or having a real family.

At her failed life, tears clouded her vision as she stumbled barefoot towards the railing off the riverfront.

*What else is there? I'm a laughingstock, a drunk, and one mean ho.*

She laughed bitterly as she recalled what Mike Lawson had called her years ago. She had never forgotten that. In light of what had just happened in Chicago, it was very appropriate.

A huge wind came and she lost her balance, going forwards over the rail. She screamed as she hit the water below. She couldn't swim.

§

Lorelei woke up in a hospital. Her head woozy and throat in pain, she tried to remember what had happened. A large nurse was beside her bed, checking some machines. When she saw Lorelei, she gave a huge grin.

"Hey hon, you finally woke up. Nod if you're feeling okay."

Lorelei opened her mouth to speak but nothing came out but acute pain. She gurgled and tried to sit up.

"Uh un, honey. Relax and don't try to speak. You've only been out of surgery for a few hours. I know it's still painful."

*Surgery? What was going on?*

"I'll be back with some pain meds after I get the doctor."

She left the room and a befuddled Lorelei tried to think. This was the second time this week she had woken up disoriented, forgetting what had happened. She knew she was in a hospital, but why? Suddenly she remembered that she was in Georgia, not Chicago…and eating at the restaurant…drinking too much and sitting at the waterfront. The nurse returned with a short, balding man whom she assumed was a doctor.

He gave a friendly smile and spoke to her as if she were a deaf child.

"Hi! Lorelei, is it? I saw it from your identification. I'm Dr. Frasier. Well, I know you're in pain but you've been through

41

a lot. After you were brought in from basically drowning in the river..."

*The hell? I almost drowned?*

"...you had a lot of fluid on your lungs, long after you were resuscitated. We couldn't get you to breathe properly and you were coughing up a little blood. After further examination, we discovered some pulmonary nodules on your lungs. You're a smoker, correct?"

Astounded, Lorelei slowly nodded.

"Okay," he said, smiling ridiculously.

*What, about any of this, was warm and fuzzy to hear? Jerk.*

"So consequently, we went ahead and performed minimally invasive emergency surgery to remove three nodules from your lungs. We felt this would improve your chances of breathing."

Lorelei started to squirm in protest. She couldn't believe what she was hearing. *Nodules on my lungs?*

Seeing her panic and confusion, he continued, "Calm down, dear. We performed a video-assisted Thorascopy," he said proudly. "In this procedure, we used a thoracoscope which is a flexible tube with a miniature camera on its end. It was inserted through a small cut into your chest wall."

Lorelei's eyes grew wide with horror. She glanced down and saw a small bandage on her chest.

"The camera allowed me to view an image of the nodules on a television screen. This technique required a smaller cut than usual and you should have a shorter recovery time than a routine thoracotomy..."

Lorelei supposed she should be thankful they didn't have to cut a huge hole in her chest.

"You were very lucky, my dear. The nodules were non-cancerous and the surgery went very well. It was my first time performing it!"

*Well, that much was clear and not helping.*

"You should be able to speak normally in a few days. Also, the CAT scan showed some scarring on your liver. Do you drink excessively?"

This time, Lorelei gave him an evil eye but nodded reluctantly.

"That's what I thought. If you don't give up drinking, you're on your way to cirrhosis of the liver. Now, Nurse Jenny here has some rehabilitation information to give you before you're released. There is a wonderful facility twenty minutes from here and as soon as you're released, I recommend admission. You drowned, dear. You should be happy and thankful to be alive," he said cheerfully.

Lorelei continued to glare at him. When Dr. Frasier figured out he wasn't going to get an enthusiastic nod, smile or anything, he wrapped it up.

"Okay, Lorelei, I'll be checking back on you in a day or two. Jenny is going to give you something for the pain. Take care."

He left and Jenny gave her a cup with two large pills to swallow. It was extremely painful. She moaned in agony which only made it worse.

"Sweetheart, you're going to have to take it easy and relax. The pain will be gone soon."

Lorelei eyed her with the most evil look she could give. She wanted to shout, *Why couldn't you just give me a shot, you big fat pig?*

# CHAPTER SIX

Two days later, Lorelei was able to speak again, although she was advised by *Nurse Portly* to whisper. She was still healing. Still weak from not using her legs, she had a hard time getting to the restroom without assistance. She saw her reflection in the mirror and more so than anything else she had just experienced - she was sure this would take her out.

Mortified, she realized she had only taken her wallet to the restaurant - no purse or cell phone - and had no access to her makeup. Thankfully, her wallet had been safe in the jacket pocket of her suit. Her hair was loose around her shoulders and was a mess. She was in dire need of a touch up.

*Good thing nobody down here knows me.*

She tried her best to comb out the snarls with the ridiculous hospital comb and brush. *Were they serious?*

Once she was back in the bed, there was a knock on the open door.

"Hello," a deeply timbered voice greeted.

She tilted her head to the side to see who was bugging her now.

*You couldn't get any rest in this place.*

Standing at the door was a man with dark brown hair dressed in hospital scrubs. Standing about six feet, he had both strong and gentle features. His eyes looked fiercely serious, yet his full soft lips were curved into a whisper of a smile. He had a strong jaw but showed signs of dimples, even though he wasn't quite smiling. He was very handsome. Her first inclination was to scream and cover up her face in shame, but she reminded herself that she didn't know him. So who cared what he thought about her? She was not in Chicago anymore. She gathered her composure and stared back in disinterest.

He came in when she didn't respond. Now he looked on the verge of laughing.

*What in the world?*

She turned her head away but it was clear he was waiting for her to respond.

After a moment, she whispered coldly, "Who are you?"

"I'm Jason Scott, a doctor here at the hospital. I just came by to see how you were."

She gave him her patented dagger stare. She knew how to make her blue eyes look intimidating and usually people cowered away, male or female. What she failed to realize was that without her excessive makeup, the result wasn't that effective.

His eyes grew, but not in intimidation. More like…amusement? Then they narrowed into something else. Recognition? He smiled and the dimples were in full effect. This guy was utterly gorgeous. Regardless of her vow of indifference, she started to get self-conscious about her appearance.

Now on defense, she whispered haughtily, "Why would you come to see me? Are you one of my doctors?"

"No, I'm not." He hesitated like he was going to say something, but thought better of it. "I'm glad you seem to be fine. I won't bother you anymore."

Curiosity burned and she couldn't help herself.

"What were you going to say?" she demanded, whisper-yelling.

He sighed. "I was the one who got you out of the water."

Speechless, she could only stare as he went on.

"My daughter and I were out on the boardwalk when we saw you in the water. It's a good thing you had on white or else you wouldn't have been noticed."

She was in shock and couldn't utter a word. The humiliation just kept on coming. A moment passed. When he saw she wasn't going to say anything else, he started backing away with his hands up.

"I'll let you get your rest. It was...nice to meet you," he glanced at her chart, "Lorelei."

Then he was gone. Shaking with rage, she stared at where he had stood for at least ten minutes. She was utterly embarrassed, incensed, mortified and any other discomforting word she could think of. *How dare* he come in here and basically laugh at her? That had to be the reason he was on the verge of laughing. Laughing because she was foolish enough to end up face down in the river. No doubt she literally looked like a drowned rat when he rescued her.

He was laughing at her - Lorelei Sampson.

Like a cold bucket of ice water on her head, that thought triggered the sex tape incident. Correction, *everyone* was laughing at her. She was more miserable than ever.

She didn't see Dr. Jason Scott anymore, and for that, she was thankful. Once she was released, she caught a cab back to the hotel where she immediately showered, careful of the area around her bandage. She had taken a peek of the wound at the hospital and saw that it was only an inch slit and was healing nicely. She applied makeup, styled her hair in her familiar up do and dressed accordingly. Now she felt better. She wanted to go back to the hospital to show *him* how gorgeous she really was. How dare he see her like that and then laugh at her. She found her mind constantly going back to that arrogant ass one way or another.

*Why am I still thinking of him?*

Instead of going out, she ordered room service and a couple of bottles of wine. *Forget what the stupid doctor said, I really need a drink.* That night she drank until she passed out.

§

The next afternoon, she found a salon and attempted to have her hair retouched to her usual blonde. Sadly, in high school, Lorelei's hair had become so damaged from home bleaching that she eventually had to have it lopped off into a short bob. Because of the many painstaking years it had taken to re-grow it, she was finally convinced to get it professionally lightened without many harsh chemicals.

Unfortunately, the stylist didn't properly heed her request today. Seeing the finished result in the mirror, Lorelei was incensed that she had dozed off in the middle of the application. She was obviously still hung-over.

"You idiot, my hair can't handle this. Why did I expect this backwards ass salon to get it right?"

"I'm so sorry, ma'am, I thought you only wanted it highlighted. It's just a light application and we conditioned it very well against breakage."

She swiveled her chair around to look directly in the woman's face.

"Did I say I wanted it highlighted? Did you hear the word 'highlight' come out of my mouth?" She got up and wrenched off the salon cape. "Just forget it."

Furious that her instructions weren't met, Lorelei threw money at the stylist and stomped out of the salon with blonde highlights. Now back at the hotel and looking in the mirror, she felt a little remorseful after cursing out the stylist.

*It actually doesn't look too bad*, she surmised before grabbing a bottle.

Other than that special outing, days passed and she'd acquired a routine. Got up, dressed to the nines, went to breakfast, came back to the room, watched reruns of *Dallas, Dynasty, Big Bang Theory* and classic old movies, ordered several bottles of wine and passed out for the rest of the night. After waking up one morning with wine colored vomit on a beautiful yellow Michael Kors dress, she knew she had a problem.

Her mother called the next day with bad news.

"Your father is still very upset with what happened and has threatened to cut you off permanently. He is extremely embarrassed and it's really uncomfortable for him when he meets with colleagues and board members. How awkward it must be for him to know that they've all seen the video of his daughter having sex - and it's displayed for the entire world to see..."

"Mallory, I know, I know. What do you want me to do? I can't undo it. By the way, I just got out the hospital."

There was a pause.

48

"What was wrong?"

"I fell into the water at the boardwalk and basically drowned. I also had emergency surgery to remove three nodules off my lungs so I could breathe better."

"Oh. Good thing you're okay."

Typical Mallory just kept going. Lorelei was accustomed to it...

"Well, he is drastically decreasing the limit of your card. You either go back to the house, which was just repaired and cleaned up today, or you come back to Chicago. I know you're going to be out of money soon."

The reality of everything hit her like a ton of bricks. Her limit was going down? She had been used to having unlimited funds for years. She had a trust but had been spending it up like crazy since she was twenty-one. It had been depleted down to the thousands and it sounded like her mother suspected as much. She was so intent on the marriage merger that she felt secure blowing her money on expensive clothes, shoes, eight hundred dollar per ounce perfume and her lavish Gold Coast condominium. This reminded her of what happened to James. She had been positively gleeful when she found out that his dad cut him off after he dumped her. Uh oh, now the shoe was on the other foot.

"Are you kidding me? I know I messed up but I'm trying to get my act together. Please - I can't come back now. I don't want to see anybody there. What can I do up there? I can't go to functions - I'll be the laughing stock of Chicago society more so than I am now if I show my face up there."

"Well then, go back to the house and stay there as long as you like. It's paid for. You need to show your father and I that you're remorseful. Maybe he'll increase your limit again."

Thinking fast, she blurted out, "Will he support me if I go to rehab?"

§

Lorelei checked into Sunny Rivers Recovery Center, twenty miles outside of Savannah. Unintentionally, she had kept the card with the information Nurse Jenny had given her. Lorelei sensed Mallory's approval and knew she would have her back when explaining it to her father. She called back later to report that Ed agreed, but still wasn't budging when it came to re-raising her limit. *Damn. Guess I'll have to work on that later...*

The first few days of detoxification were terrible and consisted of bad withdrawals. She experienced tremors, anxiety, rapid heartbeat, confusion, and was given medication to protect against other physiological aspects of withdrawal. It wasn't as bad as some of the other patients, though. She witnessed a guy across the hall having seizures and afterwards, constantly calling out in delirium. She overheard screams along the corridor and the staff having to physically detain patients. The sounds of agonized wailing started to become commonplace.

*This place sucks.*

Her symptoms lasted about a week and then she was moved to a private room that was fair. She was allowed to walk around the manicured grounds and found it pleasant enough. Initially, she hated therapy and the meetings. But what began as a way to get back in the good graces of her father became a decision she felt she must stick to. After the horrific withdrawal phase, she never wanted to go through that again. Plus, she remembered Dr. Frasier's ominous prognosis and decided to take his warning seriously.

She started to feel silly for dressing so lavishly after all of her humiliating mishaps. All it did was remind her of how stupid she had been through the years - an idiocy that culminated in a swan song on the river in an expensive Chanel suit. *How embarrassing.* Lorelei Sampson always held her head up high, no matter what - but she felt a bit chastened and ridiculous. She had been knocked down a peg or two and needed to reevaluate. She needed a complete overhaul of her life.

Therefore, for the first time in years, she toned down her style. She had purchased a few t-shirts and shorts before she checked in. Even though it was just May, it was already hot and humid in Georgia. She reasoned she had to be practical.

# CHAPTER SEVEN

On her second week, there was to be a meeting with a guest speaker. They were told the speaker was a life coach and although the teachings were more spiritual, they were useful tools anyone could use. Not really paying attention, Lorelei half listened as Marie, the main counselor, introduced the speaker.

"Today, we have someone who has been a guest life coach here for years. Please give a warm welcome to Dr. Jason Scott."

The group of twenty or so gave him alternate parts a warm or tepid welcome. Someone actually yawned loudly. Lorelei hadn't looked up yet but gave the disrespectful yawner across from her, an evil look.

Even *she* wasn't that rude…

When she looked up at the speaker, she recognized him instantly. His purposefully intent eyes were on her as well. Then he smiled with those outrageous dimples. *Oh My God….*

§

*Wow. Is that… Mean Lady from the hospital? Yep.*

She had looked so familiar to him that day, but he couldn't put his finger on where. He wanted to laugh at her expression. For some reason she amused him. Something told him that she took herself *way* too seriously.

He realized she could've been depressed after what she had been through, most patients were. But a "thank you for saving my life" wouldn't have taken much effort. That's when he figured she was a bit off. So she had a substance problem? He wondered if it was related to how he found her.

Jason hadn't been to one of these meetings in months. His small private practice, plus running in to deliver babies at the hospital had been very busy, lately. He began to speak about spiritual tools to assist in refraining from substance addiction and spoke of his own alcohol abuse. As usual, the group seemed to be surprised at his admission. Yes, he too was human and had struggled. He concluded that people were thrown off because he was a doctor. A lot of folks had the misconception that a doctor was automatically Superman - invincible and too strong willed to succumb to any kind of weakness. Granted, it had happened before he became a doctor, but since it was while he was in medical school, it could've changed the whole trajectory of his life if he hadn't gotten help.

For some reason he couldn't keep his eyes off of, what was her name? *Lorie?* She wasn't as pretty as she was in the hospital, he observed. Although dressed in casual shorts and a tee, she had on loads of makeup including loud blue eye shadow, greasy dark rouge and bright shimmery lip gloss. Her hair was lighter than before and was in some weird, elaborate style piled on the top of her head. She looked like a character from an eighties drama or something. She was still attractive, though. She looked at him with her intense blue eyes, almost as if she was trying to turn him to stone. This only made him want to laugh. He had to do everything in his power to keep from laughing out loud at this woman.

*Was she crazy?*

Since the night he rescued her out of the river, he'd been wondering whether she fell or intended to jump. That night, he and his daughter had been out together on River Street. They were walking by after leaving a hot dog stand when Abby screamed. They spotted a white figure floating in the water and he dove off the side.

Once he was able to get her onto the embankment, he went into doctor mode and performed mouth to mouth. She gurgled and spat up the water from her lungs, but coughed violently until the ambulance came and he escorted her to the hospital. It was the same hospital where a lot of his patients from his private practice gave birth. It was later that he learned emergency surgery was performed to remove some nodules from her lungs. That explained the wracking coughs.

He couldn't stop thinking about this mysterious woman after that day. What were the chances that he would see her again? He wanted to know more about her and strangely, when he saw her that day in the hospital, he was instantly drawn to her. Her glorious hair had been down around her shoulders. She had high cheekbones that didn't need any enhancements whatsoever. Most intriguing was the overwhelming despair he detected underneath her angry blue eyes. *What had she been through?* And she had looked familiar, but now she was too made up for him to really see *her*.

He scolded himself. Even today, he couldn't keep his mind on what he was saying. She was distracting.

§

After the session, he made sure to catch up with her.

"Hi, nice to see you again. What was the name? Lorie?"

She blanched at her kiddie name and all of the memories it evoked.

"No. It's Lorelei. Lorelei Sampson, if you must know," she spat.

His eyes crinkled in poorly concealed hilarity. He smiled wide. Not only was her hairstyle and makeup outdated, but she spoke like *Mommie Dearest* or somebody. *I think she watches too much TV Land.*

"I'm sorry about that. Lorelei," he corrected.

She promptly turned on her heel to make her way back to her room. He didn't try to stop her.

§

Lorelei stayed in rehab for sixty days. She thought about Jason Scott periodically and realized she had been unnecessarily rude. Normally she wouldn't have recognized her rudeness or cared, but since she was bombarded with so much self-awareness spiel around here, she couldn't help it. She even recalled some of what he had to say that day, including making restitution to those one has harmed.

*Goodness, my list is long…*

For the first time in a long time, Lorelei felt overwhelmingly guilt.

She was eligible to stay for another month but declined because she felt she was cured. She didn't want to see a glass of wine and the thought of smoking made her gag. Unfortunately, she wasn't ready to go back to any home. She was at a crossroads.

She had to admit that rehab had been a good idea for her. She felt healthier and lighter than ever. It felt good to breathe in the fresh air without any pain or craving for a smoke. She had made an acquaintance with a direct, but kind woman named Justine, who had also been addicted to alcohol. Lorelei liked her matter of fact attitude and she was as real as one could get. Justine was a far cry from the phony chicks back home. Lorelei knew because she had been one of them.

"So, you're getting out of here soon, huh?" Justine asked.

"Yeah, but I don't want to go back to Chicago or back to the place in Savannah."

Lorelei had spilled it all to Justine, figuring she didn't have anything to lose so what was the big deal? It was refreshing to be heard without an ounce of judgment. The rehab encouraged them to be honest with themselves and others. That was a major step to getting better.

"Have you checked the bulletin board? There are some postings of places for rent."

"No, I hadn't checked. Thanks."

"No problem. Take my number. Call me in another month or so. I should be all dried out, too."

They both laughed.

She took her number and promised to call. Lorelei was sincere. Another first.

§

She looked over the postings she grabbed from the board. The first one was for a tenant to board in a coach house that was on an orchard. She dialed the number but hung up quickly as she thought about it. A real orchard - like on television? She googled *orchard* on her phone and viewed some images.

*So basically like a farm. No way.*

She checked the other listings that were actually real apartments in the city. She should've known they wouldn't be available. It was looking like she was going back to the big, ugly, spooky house.

§

She had returned the Audi rental right before entering rehab. Now, she was waiting out front for a taxi when her phone rang with an unidentified number. A deep voice spoke.

"I'm sorry, I just missed a call from this number. Were you calling about the rental property?"

She wasn't sure which property they were referring to, she had called about seven places. Maybe a return call meant they were mistaken and had a vacancy?

"Yes. Do you have anything available?"

"Yes, you can come down and check it out now if you'd like. I should be here all day."

His soothing voice was accented from the south, but she detected hints of...Queens, Brooklyn...Jersey? She knew she could talk like the uppity Chicago socialite she had been, but when she was with the parents, Gino, or under pressure, she slipped back into her nasally, loud, Brooklyn voice. Not saying all Brooklynites talked like that, but she certainly did.

"Great, what's the address?"

§

She instructed the cab driver to take her to the address the guy had given her. She figured that even though the town wasn't listed as Savannah, it was probably right outside of it. It was in some place called *Sheridan*? Sunny Rivers was already a nice distance from Savannah, so imagine her surprise when the cab abruptly stopped only ten minutes away. She looked around and saw apple trees everywhere on a wide expanse of property. It looked like about fifteen acres of land.

*Oh no. Is this the orchard property listing?*

Realizing her mistake, she alerted the cab driver.

"There's been a mistake. This isn't where I thought it was..." Lorelei stopped short as she realized she had been spotted. Down the long, tree lined driveway was a large grayish house. Someone standing on the porch gave a wave. Normally she would've still taken off, but she was trying to become a kinder, gentler, more considerate, Lorelei.

"I'll be just a minute. Please wait here."

The cab driver nodded.

Inside the cab, she had no choice but to have all of her luggage with her because of the possibility that she would be returning to the big spooky house."

Today she had on white shorts, a tank top and heels. *What?* She couldn't break out of her glamorous habit totally. She was glad she was still in shape, although she had lost a few pounds in rehab.

As she got closer to the figure on the porch, she narrowed her eyes in recognition. The man was dressed in slim jeans, a fitted long-sleeved shirt that stretched across his muscular shoulders, and track shoes. He looked so *good*.

It was Dr. Jason Scott.

# CHAPTER EIGHT

He couldn't believe his eyes. The potential tenant was the mean lady, Lorie?

*You have got to be kidding me.*

He noticed that what started as a regular walk turned into a sashay as she got closer. Mmmm, she had a tight little body, though. She had obviously recognized him. Again, he wanted to laugh out loud. *She is a nutbag.*

She held out her hand. "So, we meet again. Hello, Dr. Scott."

He chuckled in surprise that she greeted him first and had remembered his name.

*So unlike the standoffish shrew from the center,* he thought pleasantly.

He internally scolded himself and cleared his throat. "Hello, Lorie." He shook her hand. He realized his mistake as soon as it came out of his mouth.

*Here we go.*

Her eyes widened in haughty disdain. She spoke between clenched teeth.

"I told you, it's Lorelei."

This time he didn't hold back and gave a full throated laugh.

Dismayed, she crossed her arms defiantly.

"What's so funny? Am I funny to you, Dr. Scott?"

"Yes, you are. You are hilarious."

"I don't see anything funny about me, but I noticed you've been laughing at me ever since that day in the hospital. Was my situation that funny?"

He sobered quickly once he realized she had misunderstood him. He had hurt her feelings.

"No, Lorelei," he said, emphasizing the correction of her name, "I wasn't laughing about anything regarding your situation. I apologize if you thought otherwise."

She straightened up and looked him up and down.

"Hmph, then what in the hell was so funny?" His eyes widened at her words and he held in his laughter.

He cleared his throat again. "It's just that you are funny to me - the way you try to look mean all of the time."

"What if I am mean?" She tried to give off a dangerous glint in her eye but he brushed it off. To him she came off more like a wounded animal. He could see the hurt in her eyes.

"Then that's too bad. You look like you have so much potential."

She was at a loss for words and didn't know how to come back. That was a new one for her.

She needed to get back on track. He distracted her, and not in a good way.

"Anyway, I'm sorry I wasted your time. I thought the listing was near Savannah, not way out here in," she looked around and waved dismissively, "in... wherever we are."

He smiled again at her snooty display. She was so funny she made his day. He didn't want to let her get away so fast. She was a nut he wanted to crack.

"Are you sure you don't want to see the property before you go? Might as well, since you're way out here already."

She considered it and thought he made logical sense.

*Oh damn, there's something else I need to do,* she thought.

"Okay. And..." Looking down, she hesitated and appeared as if she was about to sweat her way to the gas chamber.

"And...?" he prompted.

She took a deep breath while he waited.

*Geez, what was so hard to say?* Now, he was really curious.

"And... I'm...sorry for the rude way I behaved last time." She exhaled as if she had just run a marathon.

*Definitely not used to apologizing*, he thought.

He decided not to make it more uncomfortable for her than necessary. He knew she was making restitution as she'd learned in rehab.

"Apology accepted." He turned away, but not before he spotted her relieved expression. "Okay, follow me."

They walked about fifty yards off to a small two-story coach house that matched his huge one.

"It's a new construction that I had built early last year. The purpose was to have a guest house for my great aunt, but she passed away before she could move in and it's been empty. My daughter, who goes to school in Savannah, likes to hang out here from time to time. I told her not to get used to it since I'll probably be renting it out. I thought that would be the wise thing to do."

She nodded but said nothing. *Hmmm, no Mrs. Scott?*

The outside of it was interesting. It had dark grey aluminum siding that matched his house, but was a narrow, two-story construction that contained nautical windows. There was also a glass tower sitting towards the back that caught her attention. It reminded her of a designer lighthouse.

She stood back while he located the key on his massive keychain. She admired the way his shoulders rippled under his long-sleeved shirt. He was muscular, but not too much.

*And yes, he is fitting those jeans from the back…*

Blinking, she tried to get back on track.

"How do you like living way out here? Isn't it far from your work?"

"No, not really. My practice is in downtown, Sheridan." He glanced at her. "Yes, we have a downtown," he said, answering her incredulous expression. "And, as you probably figured, I'm not far from Sunny Rivers. The only place that requires a bit of a drive is the hospital. And it's not all of the time, just when my patients are about to give birth. I can get there in less than twenty minutes."

Oh, he was an obstetrician. She had wondered what his specialty was.

"Okay," she said, not sure how to respond.

For Lorelei, entering the house was love at first sight. It had a nautical sea theme throughout the first floor and it was warm and inviting. There was a fireplace and the paneled walls were all white. She could look up and see the narrow second floor and the small circular tower that was all windows. She couldn't wait to see the view. Down here was a small, but very modern kitchen with state of the art appliances. There was also a full bathroom and a small bedroom across from it.

"Since my aunt was elderly, we made sure to have a bedroom downstairs."

She nodded as they continued moving through the house, viewing the laundry room which had a trendy, cherry red washer and dryer. They made their way back towards the front where she got a better look at the living area. It was very appealing.

Her expression must have revealed her appreciation. He smiled and those dimples made her feel a bit lightheaded. She checked herself again.

*What kind of reaction is this, Lorelei? Even James didn't do this to me...Get it together.*

"It's nice, huh? I didn't decorate it. My daughter and a local decorator had their hand in this one. I just paid for everything," he said, chuckling.

"Yes, it's...charming." She tried to act reservedly but she knew she was failing. She needed to work on that. If possible, his smile widened. Was he on to her?

"Come on, let's look upstairs."

They climbed up the narrow stairs...and what she saw nearly took her breath away.

At the top of the stairs in the glass tower, there was a glorious view of his property with all of the beautiful trees and a large garden that was in the back of the house. That alone was wonderful, but when she turned her head to the right, there was a magnificent view of the ocean. It was simply spectacular. She had no idea the water could be seen from here. She was amazed.

He smiled knowingly.

"I have a tower in the other house, too. It's beautiful, isn't it?"

"Yes, yes," was all she could utter.

"Here in Sheridan, we have the best views of Tybee Island Beach off the Atlantic."

Trying to school her features from awe into one of mild interest, she nodded.

Turning her attention away from the view, he showed her the master bedroom which also had a direct view of the ocean. Her delight grew even as she tried to hide it. Jason was explaining that the queen sized bed was brand new and tested for comfort by his daughter. Surprising her even more, the master bathroom had a Jacuzzi bath. She knew she was sold but wanted to play it cool. This place was perfect for her. She put on a tight smile.

"Interesting," she mumbled.

He chuckled again but continued the tour.

"This is an extra room that we've made into a study. You can use the computer - it has wireless access, and the sofa over there is actually a pullout bed."

"Alright."

He led her back downstairs and out the front. He decided to test her since she was pretending to be undecided.

"So, I have a couple of more showings today in case you're not interested. I just had Sunny Rivers post the listing and I've been getting plenty of calls..."

That was when he saw her eyes flash in panic. He could read this lady like an open book. She might be able to fool most people, but he had her number.

"Oh no, I'll...I think I'll take it."

He smiled in satisfaction.

"Well, I don't know anything about you, Lorie, so we're going to have to talk first." He dared her to get upset about the nickname, but she wisely kept her mouth shut. *What an unexpected surprise,* he thought.

Just then, she heard the cab driver's horn. She had totally forgotten about him. But wait - wasn't she paying him? *Geez, hold your horses, buster.*

"That's right, he's waiting for me." Frustrated, she was at a loss on what to do. This was getting common lately. Dr. Scott was letting her know it wasn't automatic, and the cabbie was impatient.

"I tell you what," he drawled in a seriously, sexy voice, "send him away and if I decide you're unsuitable, I'll call another cab and pay the fare."

She could do nothing but blink.

# REMOLDED

## PART III

### CHAPTER NINE

Once they were back inside the coach house, they sat on the inviting striped Mediterranean sofa. The light blue, grey and white stripes perfectly combined to make the sofa fresh. Its color tone gave the living room such a warm coziness. There was a matching love seat across the corner and the small pillows were adorned with a tasteful starfish design. The decor gave off a romantic sea breath.

He was so ready to interrogate her. It was as if he had been waiting for this moment since he rescued her two months ago. Since that time and even after her rude behavior at the rehab, he hadn't been able to get her off his mind.

Slightly fidgeting, she looked uncomfortable under his scrutiny. He could tell she wasn't used to allowing herself to be under a microscope for anyone.

"So, Lorie...I mean Lorelei. What happened that day on the riverfront? Did you fall or were you trying..."

Appalled, she spoke indignantly, "I fell accidently, of course." She rolled her eyes at him but remembered she was trying to get his approval, not piss him off. "Thank you, by the way."

His eyes lit up in surprise. "For what?"

She sighed. He knew what. Obviously, he was going to milk it for all it was worth. She was so embarrassed and unaware that her face had turned a splotchy beet color.

"For…rescuing me." Bashful, she looked down towards the floor, no longer able to look him in the eye. This was a new one for her. "I really appreciate it."

He softened at her words. She seemed to be really trying.

"You're welcome." Sensing her unease, he decided to let her off the hook once again by changing the subject.

"Lorelei, where are you from?"

"I'm from Chicago."

"Not originally. You have a New York accent, specifically, Brooklyn."

Amazed that he had detected it, she rounded on him and completely let it out, sounding just like Howard's mom on *The Big Bang Theory*.

"You've got some nerve. I detect hints of Jersey from you!"

He laughed heartily. He knew she was hilarious. He laughed for a full minute before he could speak. She actually laughed, too.

"You picked up on my accent? I thought I only had a southern twang left since I've been down here for over thirteen years. But you're right. I lived in Jersey and then we moved to Brooklyn when I was fourteen."

Without giving too much away, she explained that she moved to Chicago from Brooklyn in her teens.

They looked at each other in amazement. Then he pulled out his old dialect.

"Show me a beautiful broad (pronounced brod) and I'll show you a guy that's tired of doin' her."

They both laughed uproariously. She couldn't remember the last time she had laughed so hard.

§

Jason told her that he was planning to rent to a female only and would've rejected her if he called back and she was a guy. It was the first and only place he had posted the listing. He wanted to help out former women patients more so than men because he felt men adapted easier out in the elements. He could tell Lorelei was pretty tough, though. She gave him an abbreviated summary of her background and affiliation with Sampson Electronics, to which he listened with interest, but didn't pry. Lorelei appreciated that. She didn't want him to know too much about her…

They talked about rent, utilities and other pertinent information he thought she might need to know and then gave her a set of keys. After he left, Lorelei contentedly got settled into the quaint little house. It was the perfect size for her. It was light and airy, brand new, and had the most beautiful views. The only problem was that although the rent was reasonable, she would be low on money in a matter of months. While she knew she could dig into what was left of her trust, she didn't want to go down to zero. She hoped her father would raise her limit again, soon.

She lay in the bed that she made up with fresh fragrant sheets from the linen closet. He had informed her that a housekeeper came in once a month to wash, dust and clean the place. Since he made no mention of a wife, she assumed he was divorced or a single baby daddy or something.

She could see the view right from the bed. It was so soothing. It was much like her view of Lake Michigan, which was what she missed the most about her abandoned condominium. Along with that thought came a knotted stomach as she painfully recalled what had happened in Chicago. She felt like she was in another dimension down here in rural Georgia on an apple orchard. She had to think about that twice. *Her, Lorelei Sampson, down south on an apple orchard?*

§

That evening, she watched the television in the living room and eventually retired upstairs. Just seeing the tranquil, clear night where the stars were visible, calmed her. The place wasn't big enough for her to feel spooked. Now that she thought about it, her condo wasn't that big either. So, of course she wouldn't be content staying in that huge mansion by herself. Here, she was very comfortable. And she knew Jason Scott wasn't far away…

She slept until late the next morning. When she awoke, she couldn't believe it was already ten o'clock. She had been used to rising early at rehab and this was unusual. Due to the anxiety of blindly figuring out her next move, she had been exhausted.

Just before she styled her hair and applied her makeup, she heard a light tap on the door.

Embarrassed about being caught without her makeup, she hesitated, not sure what to do. It had to be Jason Scott. Who else knew she was here?

The tapping repeated and was more insistent. With no choice, she went down to open the door.

His eyes looked at her with an expression she hadn't seen in a while. It was genuine appreciation.

*What was his problem?*

He said nothing for a moment, then seemed to remember why he was here.

"Good Morning."

She hesitated, skeptical that this was the sole reason for his visit.

"Good Morning."

"I just came to tell you I'm leaving for work." He looked at his watch. "I usually leave much earlier but I have late appointments this afternoon. What do you have planned for today?"

Embarrassed, she wasn't sure how to answer. She really didn't have anything to do. To save face, she made up something fast.

"Well, I have some phone calls to make back to Chicago, and once I saw the washer and dryer, I realized I have a lot of washing to do..."

His smirk showed that he was on to her.

"Can't all of that wait? Want to take a ride with me?"

Thrown off guard, she blanched. She hadn't seen that invitation coming.

Totally out of character, Lorelei stuttered, "Where to?"

"Come and see downtown Sheridan and my practice."

Admitting to herself that she really had nothing better to do, she gave in.

"Well, okay. Let me finish getting ready."

He couldn't help himself, he had to stop her.

"Lorie, you look great, now. You don't need to do anything but come on. You look so much younger with your hair down and you don't need all of that makeup."

Her eyes grew big in offense.

*How dare he?*

"Well, I've never! That was so rude."

Realizing he had completely offended her, he tried to smooth it over. But not before he chuckled at her old fashioned response. He held up his hands.

"I'm sorry, forgive me. It's just that you're such a beautiful woman, just like the woman I saw that day in the hospital. You have the most striking bone structure. How old are you?"

Astounded, she sputtered, her mouth opening and closing like a dying fish.

"You are very impolite! Now you're asking me my age? Does your rudeness know no bounds?"

He laughed heartily. This woman needs help.

"Are you thirty? Thirty-one?" When she didn't answer, he knew how to get a response. "Thirty-five?"

"No! I'm only thirty-one," she answered indignantly.

"That's what I thought, same age as me. Anyway, you look like you're in your low twenties without all of that...cak-...uh - makeup on your face. Like most women, I'm sure you want to look younger, right?"

"I am certainly *not* most women!"

"That's for sure," he mumbled under his breath, but she heard it.

She looked at him in bewilderment, shaking her head.

"Dr. Scott, you need to think before you speak. There are certain things you should never ask a woman."

"I'm sorry, you got me." He put up his hands in surrender. "I'm guilty for speaking my mind. I apologize, Lorie."

"I told you, it's Lorelei!"

He waved his hand dismissively and she gasped.

"Alright, Lorelei - I'll be in the car. You've got ten minutes, hurry up."

Before she could retort, he abruptly turned and strode confidently towards a dark blue SUV, his swag out of control. Meanwhile, her mouth was wide open. He was trying to boss her around, too?

She hurriedly closed the door, leaning against it. She breathed in deep breaths to slow down her heartbeat. She had never met a man that could garner this type of response from her. He was brutally honest and obviously didn't adhere to any of the social mores of elite society. Where *were* his manners? His filter?

She thought about him as she made her way up to the bathroom to get her face and hair together. Once she got to the mirror, she studied her appearance, involuntarily considering his suggestions. Did she look younger the way she was right now? She tried to look at herself objectively, the way a man might see her. She always thought that men liked the way she styled herself. She saw how they reacted to her favorite heroine's on her favorite syndicated shows and classic movies...

*Could my style be (gasp!)...outdated?*

She looked closer. He said she looked like she was in her twenties. Despite all of his bluntness, that was one comment she didn't mind hearing. Deciding not to totally let him have the upper hand, she pulled her hair back in a ponytail instead leaving it loose. Instead of a fully made up face, she only added a dusting of powder, eyebrow pencil to give shape, and lipstick. Her eyebrows had been growing back since she'd left Chicago. She had decided to try a different look instead of having them totally waxed off and drawn on. She felt her Marlene Dietrich look had run its course.

However, she missed her expensive 1929 perfume, *Joy* by Jean Patou. She would practically bathe in the stuff, but now she had to budget. It was probably just as well since she started having massive breakouts; maybe she used too much? Her discovery of Shea butter and baby oil was an epiphany.

She surveyed herself once more in the mirror. She had to say she liked the look. It reminded her of the carefree way the young girls wore their hair and makeup today. She always thought they looked plain and uninteresting, but she could see how it would fit better with this climate and her new casual way of dressing. Was this another change for Lorelei Sampson?

Today, she had on a salmon colored tank under a sheer white blouse and white capris. On her feet were bejeweled, low wedge sandals. She had always worn high heels to accommodate her short stature, but dangit - she had to admit these were comfortable. She ignored the real reason she hadn't styled her hair and makeup the usual way – because *he* told her not to...

Once she climbed her five foot frame up into the passenger seat, his eyes blatantly looked her up and down, missing nothing.

"You look very nice, Lorie."

Putting on her sunglasses, she sighed at his familiar name usage, too fatigued to fight.

"I guess this is going to be a habit of yours - one I don't feel like constantly correcting, but thank you, Dr. Scott."

"Please, call me Jason," he said, grinning.

# CHAPTER TEN

Downtown Sheridan was just as she thought it would be - quaint, charming, lots of small storefronts, including an ice cream parlor, a coffee shop and trolley cars. She admitted she had always liked cobblestone streets. He pulled up into a parking lot that was next to the coffee shop. She read the sign:

*River Valley Women's Health and Obstetrics. Dr. Jason D. Scott, Dr. Lillian A. Montague, Dr. Peter J. Mansfield.*

He answered her inquisitive expression.

"I run this facility along with another obstetrician, a gynecologist and a midwife."

*Midwife, they still have those?*

"Dr. Montague and I work together as a team because there are times when one of us will be at the hospital assisting in the delivery of a baby. In that instance, she can see a patient during a prenatal visit. The midwife also helps assist the expectant mothers, and in a lot of cases are more hands on and accessible than us. Come inside."

Once inside the very well kept clinic, she was introduced to a young receptionist that looked at Lorelei like she was from outer space.

"Hey, Rebecca, this is my friend, Lorelei."

At least he used her full name. *Friend, huh?* Secretly, she liked it.

Lorelei did everything in her power not to give the chick her patented death glare. She was trying to be more affable, right? This was the new Lorelei.

She reached out her hand and spoke gloriously. "Hello, Rebecca. A pleasure to meet you."

"Hi," Rebecca responded vacantly.

Jason was smiling that secret smile again like he wanted to laugh.

She looked at him in confusion. What? What had she done?

They walked on and Jason whispered conspiratorially,

"They're not used to me bringing a guest, so please excuse them."

His colleague, Dr. Lillian Montague, was a striking woman with a beautiful brown complexion that looked to be in her late forties. She had a friendly smile and welcomed Lorelei, holding out her hand.

"Hello, Lorelei, pleased to meet you. Dr. Scott never brings a visitor, so please forgive everyone if they're curious. I know I am." She giggled.

*Did these folks down south have no decorum and no shame?*

Lorelei sighed inwardly. She didn't know how long she would be down here, but if she didn't want to become a recluse in her new ivory tower, she'd better make some changes.

*I guess if you can't beat em, join em.*

She attempted to laugh along. Jason laughed heartily at her attempt.

Lorelei was admittedly nervous on how he would explain their acquaintance.

"Lorie is from my home town and was just down here visiting. She's staying in my coach house for a little while."

*Pretty good*, she thought. *Vague, but pretty good.*

If anything, that only made Dr. Lillian extra curious.

"Really, is she an old friend from high school or something?"

Jason looked at Lorelei and smiled widely, his mind clicking.

"Why, yes. Yes, she is."

§

She didn't know why he felt the need to embellish, but whatever worked. She was just thankful he didn't sell her out as a pathetic drowning victim that doubled as a raging alcoholic.

*These folks were nosy as all hell...*

Not to mention what had happened in Chicago. *Oh no. What if he knows what happened in Chicago?* She hadn't thought about that.

She was introduced to a cordial, slender young woman named Rose, who was surprisingly, the midwife. Lorelei didn't know why, but when she thought of the term midwife, she thought of an older, heavy-set woman named Helga or something. Too much TV.

He informed her that the gynecologist, Dr. Mansfield, was at the hospital today.

*I need a gynecologist down here*, she thought. She'd had the foresight to get checked out and tested not too long after ending things with the slimeball, thank goodness, but if she was going to be down here for any length of time, she was going to need one.

They headed back to the house so he could drop her off. They both remained silent for the five minute drive. He pulled the car in front of the coach house.

"It isn't very busy today and I only have two appointments this afternoon. So, what did you think?" He asked, dimples blinding her

She blinked as she tried to get her bearings. He was disarming her, minute by minute. Nobody disarmed Lorelei Sampson - nobody, not even James. Not even Mike Lawson did this.

She attempted to compose herself. "Well, I thought it was very interesting. It seems… you have a very nice practice."

He smiled widely.

"Thank you, Lorie. I can really call you that now, right?" His eyes were intently searching hers. They laser focused into her own, as if he was breaking her, controlling her. Did he have some type of mystical power?

"Yes," she said, almost trance-like. She couldn't' believe what had just come out of her mouth and turned away abruptly, grabbing the car door handle.

"I've got to go."

She ran out of the car and to the door of the coach house. She fumbled in her purse for the keys but couldn't find them. She looked towards the SUV where Jason stood outside of the car holding up the set of keys. He had a sexy smirk on his face.

"They must've fallen out of your purse."

Mortified, they met halfway and he handed her the keys. His hand touched hers and it scorched her skin, giving her goose bumps. Why was he affecting her like this?

"Thanks." She turned around, unlocked the door and hurriedly entered the house. Closing the door, she leaned against it, her breaths uneven. She was totally flabbergasted by her response to him.

§

The next day, there was another knock around the same time as yesterday. She was already up and dressed in jean shorts and a tank. She had checked the weather which reported that it would be very humid.

She opened the door and sure enough, it was Jason. He was dressed way too casually with shorts and a tee shirt...and that disarming smile. Wow, he was gorgeous. His eyes traveled the length of her, paying close attention to her minimally made up face and ponytailed hair, which according to the appreciative gleam, was acceptable. It made her a bit testy that he was scrutinizing her.

"Why *are* you looking at me like that? Do I look okay?" She asked, rolling her eyes and neck with her hand on her hip.

He laughed. "Good Morning to you too, Lorie. Of course. You look more than okay."

She smirked, "Glad I passed your test."

He couldn't help but laugh again. "You're silly. There isn't any test - I just think you're naturally beautiful."

Lorelei didn't know she was so capable of blushing anymore, but she did.

He stared at her a beat too long, and then remembered why he was at her door this morning.

"I don't have any scheduled appointments and was wondering if you wanted to take another drive with me?"

She shrugged. "I guess."

§

They took a short drive and ended up at the beach. She was pleasantly surprised and it showed on her face.

"Wow," she exclaimed in awe.

She never took her eyes off the water while he parked the car. He chuckled at her reaction and studied her with an inquisitive smile, wondering about everything that was going through the head of this strange woman. She was such an enigma. Cold and haughty one moment, happy and childlike the next.

They got out and walked towards the serene blue water. The beach on Tybee Island was a twenty minute drive from Savannah, but from Sheridan, only seven minutes. There were miles of beautiful beach, forts and a museum. But what stood out most was a massive black and white lighthouse. It was magnificent.

"That lighthouse, called *The Tybee Island Light*, is one of seven surviving colonial era lighthouse towers. It was first built in 1736, but reconstructed several times in the 1800's."

"How tall is it?"

"It's one hundred forty-four feet."

There were also ocean front cottages lined along the beach. There weren't a lot of people out since it was still fairly early. They walked alongside the water, Jason

81

periodically skipping rocks. It was tranquil and very relaxing.

She walked with her hands in her pockets, looking deep in thought but with a look of peace. After a few minutes, she took off her sandals and enjoyed the feeling of the sand beneath her feet and between her toes. She felt young and carefree. She turned to see what he was doing and he was staring at her, his mouth slightly parted as if he was trying to figure her out. She casually turned her head back to the water. She didn't know what his problem was, but she was enjoying herself too much to care right now.

"You love the ocean, don't you? I noticed a similar reaction when you saw the view from the coach house."

He watched as incredibly, her face morphed into a remote mask. Maybe she was reminded of that night…

"It's… nice."

He was intrigued at the way she shut down. He was going to figure her out if he did nothing else.

"You know I remember you."

A look of unease flashed across her face as she sharply turned her head towards him, almost faltering in her steps. Had he seen the video? Her heart stuttered.

"What do you mean?" she asked guardedly.

"I remember you when we were younger. Didn't you go to Liberty High in Brooklyn?"

Her eyes grew big in her sockets. She looked at him closely, trying to see him fifteen years ago. He did look familiar. She was terrified. He probably remembered all of the dirt she performed in high school.

Nervously, she looked down at her hands and began fidgeting. She was ashamed.

"What's wrong, Lorie? You did, didn't you?"

He couldn't figure out why she was so unsettled by the revelation. What was the big deal?

"Yes, I went there, for my freshman and sophomore year and then I... transferred out."

"I thought so!" he smiled widely. "I didn't get there until I was a sophomore. Remember – I told you we moved from Jersey when I was fourteen going on fifteen." He smiled and laughed happily.

Maybe that was a good thing. That meant there was only one year that they were at Liberty at the same time. Maybe he wasn't at Liberty long enough to know of her horrible reputation because she left soon after that. She hoped this was the case.

She said nothing as they continued walking, looking far off into the distance. In contrast, he was jubilant that his assumption was correct and walked with a skip in his step.

"I usually never forget a face and I knew it as soon as I saw you in the hospital. It didn't click until I was introducing you at the office."

She turned to look at him in amazement.

"So, you realized it then? When you told them I went to your high school? I thought you were making that up."

"Yes. I knew it - right then. At that very moment, I could see your face when we were younger. And I knew that's where it was from." He looked at her closely. "Do you remember me?" he asked quietly.

She stopped walking and studied his features. There were so many guys that she really didn't take a good look at back then. She could imagine that he was probably as good looking as he was now.

"I think so. You look familiar, now that I look at you." She didn't want to divulge that she had probably slept with him and didn't remember.

"I was much shorter back then." He smiled like he had a huge secret. "You know what I remember about you, Lorie?"

She was terrified to hear the answer. "What?" she asked apprehensively.

He moved in real close, looking down at her intently.

"I remember I liked you and I think we even went out."

*Oh no.*

# CHAPTER ELEVEN

She wracked her brain trying to remember a shorter *Jason Scott* in high school, but she couldn't. She thought she remembered someone who may have looked like him, but she wasn't sure. She was such a basket case back then that it was no use.

Thankfully changing the subject, he pointed out some of the attractions including a museum that he said they must visit on another day. They walked a long distance and were on their way back towards the car. She fiddled around with her ponytail and unwittingly broke the band. Her hair cascaded down around her shoulders. She tried to put it in a knot but a hand came out, stopping her.

"Leave it. I want to see it down."

She wasn't going to let him think he could control her every move. Ignoring him, she continued trying to knot it.

"But it's a mess out here in the breeze…"

"Exactly. Lorelei, I said leave it," he demanded gently. "Please."

Taken aback by his fervent request using her full name, her hands slowly fell down to her sides.

He smiled triumphantly and studied her. She wanted to flinch under his perusal.

"Your hair, do you color it?"

*There he goes again with these personal questions.*

"If you must know, yes," she responded with attitude. She should've known by now that it still wouldn't deter him.

"What color is it really? Is it the light brown color I see inside the streaks? The color I saw at the hospital?"

"Sort of." She rounded on him. "Why?" she demanded, incredulous at his inquiry. He was so intrusive.

"Because it looks very soft… and very pretty. I liked it and it's nice like this, too. But don't color it so much. You're a natural beauty."

She wasn't mistaken that he was openly flirting so she had a personal question of her own.

"Jason, where is Mrs. Scott?"

He looked taken aback but smoothly recomposed his features. "There isn't a Mrs. Scott."

"Oh." Why was she so relieved? Why did she even care?

He continued to study her hair. In spite of herself, she blushed again. Although it was warm outside, she shivered as he stepped closer, reaching out to touch a few strands.

After a moment he murmured, "I love the feel of your hair."

She was frozen like a frightened animal as he closed in and turned her around to face him. He put his hands in her hair, stroking it to the ends.

Her heart was ready to beat out of her chest. His actions seemed innocent enough, but she had never experienced something so sensual. And all he was doing was touching her hair.

Realizing the response he was evoking, he continued stroking it. Her eyes closed of their own accord and she succumbed to his ministrations. Just then, a wave of tenderness that he hadn't felt in years towards a woman, overcame him. *Poor little baby needs some affection,* he thought.

He wanted to choke up as he realized that this little lamb just needed somebody to care for her. Her tough girl façade was just that, a façade. That was her defense against the world because she had been burnt. He could just feel it.

Watching her serene, relaxed face, he experienced something akin to déjà vu. He couldn't put his finger on it, but she reminded him of someone else, too...

He put his hands up into her scalp and began massaging her head. She moaned. *Mmm, that sounds good*, he thought. Just then, her eyes jumped open as she realized what she was doing. She was losing control. She jerked away from him and continued walking. He chuckled and followed.

She cleared her throat.

"I have some things I need to do back at the house. I really do need to wash today." Not looking back, she stomped faster towards his car which was coming into view.

He was amused that she needed an excuse to get away from him, but he didn't press.

"No problem."

They were silent on the short trip back to his estate. He pulled into his drive and she made her way over to the coach house.

Remembering some manners, she called out, "Thank you for showing me the beach. It was beautiful."

"No problem. Next time we can actually get in the water."

He chuckled when she ignored him.

§

Once inside, she marched to the bathroom to wash the remaining sand off of her legs.

Again, she tried to understand her response to Jason Scott. She had never let any man disarm her so completely. She was in a virtual trance when he caressed her hair on the beach. And when he started stroking her scalp, she'd become someone else. She felt like she was responding to him like those silly girls from the stupid romance novels she rarely read. Or one of those fawning females from the shows she watched. Although she enjoyed watching them, she prided herself that no guy had ever made her blood race or her heart melt or any of that baloney. Not even Mike Lawson or James did this. After all, he was just a man and she knew how to deal with men...

Now ashamed that he remembered her and that they possibly dated (or more), she was reminded about the video scandal. What if he looked her up on Liberty High's yearbook page and found a discussion of her and the sex tape? *Oh my goodness! What if he finds the video?*

Petrified, she immediately called the head of their IT Department, Josh, who had been personally assisting her with the matter. She hadn't talked to him since rehab where he assured her that the video was down and there hadn't been any traces of it. She couldn't stand to be reminded of that dreaded incident but she needed reassurance.

He answered in one ring. "Hello, Ms. Sampson."

"It that video removed for good?" she spat out without preamble.

"Yes, it's removed. It was reposted a few times, but my team and I are on it just in case it comes back."

"What? It's been reposted a *few* times?" Her hands were trembling as she held the phone to her ear.

This was devastating news. That meant it could be reposted over and over as she was sure copies were being made.

"Um…yes?"

She screeched, "Make for damn sure it doesn't return or I'll have you and your whole crew fired!"

He was silent.

"Do you freakin' hear me?" she demanded when he didn't respond.

"Yes, Ms. Sampson. We'll do everything in our power to make sure it is taken down permanently."

She hung up the phone. *Oh My Goodness, I need a drink!*

Lorelei flew into the kitchen and tore open every empty cabinet looking for some semblance of booze. Finding none, her mind raced.

*I can call a taxi to take me to a liquor store…*

Conscious that she was behaving like a maniac, she tried to calm down.

*I can't go back to that. Just remember rehab and the withdrawals. It was awful. I'm in control. I am in control of my body, not my body in control over me…*

She sat on the sofa, rocking back and forth for hours. She tried to recall the twelve steps and repeated them. Every time she recited them, along came the image of her face plastered on the big screen at The Drake. Her face contorted…ugh, how humiliating. And then all eyes on her. She screamed out loud in shame. She kept rocking and reciting, trying to block out the images with her voice.

When she finally looked at the old fashioned analog clock on the wall, it was three o' clock. She had been sitting there for hours trying to fight a relapse.

*He should be home, right?*

She looked at her phone and found the number she had used to call regarding the property. Should she call? Lorelei had never needed anyone but she had been feeling so vulnerable lately. This was all new to her. She really needed to talk to someone and after all, he was a life coach. She contemplated for about five minutes, and then dialed his number.

"Hello?"

"Hello, Jason? This is Lorelei."

"Hey, Lorie, what are you up to?"

She could hear the smile in his voice and immediately, she relaxed.

"I was wondering… could you come over here to… talk?"

# ENLIGHTENED

## PART IV

### CHAPTER TWELVE

After letting Jason in, they sat on the sofa. He was instantly on alert when he saw her face.

"Jason, I hope I didn't interrupt anything. It's just that I needed...I needed..." She trailed off and uncharacteristically, burst into tears.

Lorelei covered her face in shame, and with long hiccupping sobs, wept bitterly. He gathered her into his arms. It felt so good to be held. She didn't know how long she stayed there, but weeping wasn't something she had done since she was a teenager. She had certainly cried back at her condo, but usually stopped the torrent with resolve, a cigarette, or a drink. Something to drown out...*feelings*. She usually didn't allow herself to fall completely apart. That wasn't her modus operandi.

She released all of her feelings of frustration, despair and the mess she'd made of her life and other's lives.

"Jason..." she wailed. "I'm such a horrible, horrible person. I've done so many horrible things to so many people..."

He patted her back, consoling and shushing her.

She adamantly shook her head.

"No, you've got to let me finish. I have...I have done such awful things - you should've left me in the water that night. I didn't deserve to...live," she hiccupped.

"No, that's not true. Of course you deserve to live. Everyone deserves a second chance." She pushed away from him, looking up into his handsome face, willing him to understand.

"No, no, no. You don't understand. I don't deserve to live. I've almost...killed people." She looked up in his intense eyes, seeing if she had shocked him. His expression didn't change.

"We've all done things we aren't proud of. Human beings are capable of virtually anything. That's why we need to succumb to a higher power."

This sounded like some of the things he had said in the group meeting. Whatever... it was soothing. She nestled back into his good smelling arms and listened. She had to admit that she felt like a lost newborn. She had lived her life a certain way for so long, thinking it was right. Now she realized she had been dead wrong all along.

"We are all a creation and since Adam's fall in the garden, we took on a sin nature. That disobedience in the garden separated us from our Creator. The only way to truly be at peace is letting the Creator back into your life and living His way."

Instead of being turned off like she had in the past about any religious type of chatter, she was intrigued. With the way her life was, it was obvious she knew nothing - because it was a mess. She needed help in any way she could get it.

Feeling a strange bond with this man whom she had just met again yesterday, she opened up.

"Jason. For some reason I feel I can talk to you..."

She sat facing him with her head down and confessed about her bullying over the years starting from ten, her reckless behavior with men, her two failed engagements solely for money's sake, the despicable incident where she drugged, beat up and dumped James's mistress on a bad side of town, and the latest debacle in Chicago. She left almost nothing out. He listened quietly and without judgment. Once she was done, she looked up at him, ready to flinch at what she would find. Instead of shocked ridicule, it contained compassion and not...pity.

"Your story sounds like countless other stories I've heard. It's not unique. You just lost your way."

Looking at him in wonder, she was speechless.

"No way, Jason. Did you hear what I just told you? I behaved wickedly."

He smirked, shaking his head. "Yeah, I admit that sounded pretty jacked up, but let me ask you this. What was the one thing you craved when you were a child? Was it a new doll, a new bike, the latest video game?" he asked.

She thought about her answer. Even though it came instantly, she wondered if she should cover up the truth. She would feel so exposed. She had never admitted it to anyone.

"I wanted... lots of hugs from my mother and father. I wanted to call my mother, *mom* - but she never let me. Like *The Brady Bunch*, I wanted a family just like that."

"That's what I guessed. You craved affection and didn't get it. That's probably why you slept around. It's understandable, Lorie. Not right, but understandable. Your first bullying was in fourth grade when the girl took the swing out from under you. Was she bigger than you?"

"Yes, I was always very little."

"You had to assert yourself as a young girl and felt you had no backup because your parents either weren't home or didn't have time for you. Your case is almost textbook. Again, I'm not condoning your behavior, because you truly did some awful stuff," he laughed and she cringed, "but it's understood."

Afterwards, she felt as if a great big weight had been lifted. She had finally told someone most of her secrets, and he was still sitting here, being non-judgmental. Telling her that she could be forgiven.

"Go to church with me, Sunday."

§

For the next few days, Lorie stayed home trying to read a Bible that was on one of the shelves in the study. She didn't understand what she was reading but she received a peace. She needed time to reflect on herself and make some changes.

That Sunday, she went to church with Jason. The pastor taught that we all needed redemption and that with a new life in Christ, we would be born again with a new life into a new kingdom. No matter what bad we had done. She didn't know how much of that she believed but she knew she needed to believe something. She couldn't grasp that there was a God willing to forgive all of her dastardly deeds, but when the pastor called for people to come and receive the free gift of salvation, she stood up and gave her life to Christ. Jason was ecstatic.

Afterwards, she didn't feel anything had changed and in truth, still wanted a drink. She told Jason of these feelings.

"That's normal."

"But I don't feel anything."

"That's the problem - we go by our five senses too much. You are a new creation whether you can feel it or not. Your body is still the same and even your mind. But you have a new spirit. And now the hard part comes. You have to put that flesh under subjection. You have to renew your mind."

"What does that mean?"

"That means that you've been programmed to live and think a certain way that is consistent with the world's way, or the devil's way. The new way to think is according to God's way of doing things. Or, to *seek first the kingdom of God*, that's Matthew 6:33 - *and all these things shall be added to you*."

"I don't get it."

"You have to be kingdom minded. That means seeking God's way in every problem that may occur. You need healing, you can speak healing over you and others with just your voice and the Word of God and you will recover. But that requires faith. Of course, being a doctor, I believe in doctors and medicines, but there is a higher alternative. Don't get me wrong, thank God for modern medicine. Without it, a lot of people, including Believers, would be dead. But God will meet you where you are. Matthew 9:29 say, *According to your faith, be it unto you.* He'll meet you according to your faith."

She nodded while he continued.

"To conquer alcohol and other substance abuse, you can speak a verse and be delivered like I was from it. Galatians 5:1 says, *Stand firm with the liberty that Christ has set you free and not be entangled by the yoke of bondage again.* Meditating on that verse made me lose the desire for alcohol, right away. It actually made my nose detest the smell. Isn't that amazing? Plus, we have to continually walk in the spirit so that we don't fulfill the lust of the flesh. It's not easy and I struggle with it...in other ways..." he trailed off.

Now quiet, she could guess what he meant. Something in his expression told her not to ask right now. She deflected by reading the rest of the verse again.

"What are the so called "things that shall be added unto you? Money?"

"That's not just talking money, but total prosperity. The word prosperity includes health, peace of mind, provision, fulfillment and everything else good you can think of. But it's not simple at first because you renew your mind by building your faith in God's Word. We all have been given the same measure of faith, as Pastor Murphy taught Sunday, but we have to develop it. The only way to do that is to stay in the Word of God. Romans 10:17 says, *Faith comes by hearing, and hearing the Word of God."*

Jason and Lorelei had bible study every evening at the coach house. She was serious about learning about God and His Word.

It was amazing to him how the people who behaved the worst or had a serious weakness were the easiest to come to Christ. It was always the ones that thought they had it all together and were successful in life that were the hardest to budge. He was amazed at Lorelei's enthusiasm.

But he also knew that if she hadn't gone through what she had gone through, she would probably still be in Chicago, raising hell.

§

The following week, Jason showed Lorelei around the orchard. He cultivated Gala, Honeycrisp, Red Delicious, and Fuji apples. He sold them to a few surrounding canneries and farmer's markets in Georgia that made apple based products like sauce, juice, cider, apple butter, pies and other desserts. With Jason's fluctuating schedule, he couldn't really devote much time to the business of the orchard, but it meant too much to him to shut it down. The farm was passed down in the family.

He had an aging fellow named Duke that came in to take care of the business for him. Duke managed the orchard by spraying, pruning, and general maintenance. He harvested the apples, delivered them to clients, collected the money and gave Jason his profit. Although now that Duke was getting up in age, he wasn't able to do as much labor. Jason was in the process of looking for help for old Duke. Usually, Abby, Jason's daughter was around to help but she was away at school.

Jason talked about Abby with so much affection.

"How old is your little girl?"

"She's fifteen going on sixteen."

For some reason Lorelei envisioned an eight or nine year old. "Really?"

"Yeah. Actually, she's fifteen going on thirty," he chuckled. "She begged last year to go to a boarding school in Savannah - I guess things were a little too slow for her down here. She calls all of the time, though. I think she worries about her old man," he said, chuckling.

Lorelei smiled. "What's she like?"

"She's beautiful, strong willed, brilliant and fiercely determined."

"Where's her mom?"

He hesitated as a shadow fell over his face.

"Things didn't work out, and Gina and I were divorced seven years ago."

"Sorry to hear that. Did Abby take it hard?"

"Not as hard as I thought. She's one tough cookie."

Deciding to change the subject because she could sense it was a sore subject for him, she reached up and picked an apple.

"Show me how to pick apples."

## CHAPTER THIRTEEN

Surprised, she found out she rather enjoyed it. Therefore, certainly doing something she had never done before, Jason and Duke showed Lorelei how to harvest the best apples for the apple orchard business. *Her, Lorelei Sampson.* She was paid a wage by Jason, one that was well over the picking of a few bushels of apples, but she appreciated and accepted it just the same. It would help offset her rent. She'd come to enjoy being out in nature. She'd read a few of the garden books that were up in the study and even started tending to the garden out back.

The following Sunday, Lorelei officially joined church and got baptized. Over the next few weeks, she and Jason's friendship grew and they had developed a bit of a routine. He went to work while she worked with Duke, picking apples during the day. She had a few recipes up her sleeve and cooked dinner for Jason about three nights a week. He let her use his extra car if she needed to go into town to the store. After dinner, they had bible study. She was getting used to this sedentary life. She truly felt as if she was brand new.

One night, he called her just ten minutes after he left. She had been curious about his chosen career for a while.

"Why did you decide to become an obstetrician?"

"When I was a freshman in college, I was studying in the library and a woman went into labor right there...this baby was coming fast, and the paramedics weren't there yet.

Along with another woman, I helped deliver her baby, right there on the library floor. I experienced so much joy helping to bring that precious life into the world. That's when I knew what I wanted to do."

She was quiet.

"You still there?"

"Yes."

"Was there something you always wanted to do? What did you dream of becoming when you were younger?"

She tried to think back to what her goals were before Ed and Mallory made it a family ambition for her to be a gold digger.

She giggled because she had never told anyone.

He laughed, "Tell me. I won't laugh."

"You're laughing now."

"Only because you're laughing. I haven't heard that sound a lot - and I like it."

She blushed.

"Tell me," he insisted.

"Okay. When I was younger, I dreamed of becoming a ballerina. I thought I was suitable enough because I was so small. And with my hair up in a ponytail, I looked just like the young ballerinas I saw on television. I remember begging my mother for lessons but she wouldn't let me go...telling me it was trivial bull..." Her voice trailed off.

He was quiet for a moment.

"Sorry that you didn't get a chance to do that. I bet you would've made a beautiful ballerina."

She had received plenty of compliments from men, but usually because they wanted something in return. For the first time, she felt a man was being sincere, just because.

"Thanks," she said awkwardly. She wasn't used to just talking to a guy she liked on the phone like this. It was all new to her.

"Did you go to college?" he asked.

"Yes, I graduated from Loyola University in Chicago with a BBA degree in finance. My parents thought it would be best to learn about money. That's what the Sampson's were all about. Making dollars," she said, laughing bitterly.

He chuckled along. After a moment he asked quietly, "What would you rather have majored in?"

She sighed. "Deep down, I was interested in a career in nursing. I know it's silly, but I had a lot of dolls when I was about five or six. And because my parents were always away, they were my family. I imagined that they were sick at various times and I cared for them like I was nurse."

"Really?" he said, amazed. "That's not silly. That's how a lot of people find out what they really want to do in life. It starts from somewhere. I never would've guessed that."

"Yep," she said, her lip popping the p.

§

Jason came over the next evening. As they finished bible study, he stretched out his legs.

"Miss Lorie, I could get used to this. Your smothered pork chops were divine. Where in the world did you learn that recipe?"

101

She laughed happily. "In addition to the TV shows that I love, I watch cooking shows. I got this recipe from your local treasure, Ms. Paula Deen."

"Really? I should've known."

He had been going directly to the love seat, lately. She had hoped it meant what she thought it meant, but she didn't want to get too hopeful. Over the last few weeks, she had a wonderful, growing friendship with Jason that she didn't want to ruin.

She wasn't used to being friends with a guy, without either: A) Attempting to jump his bones for affection, B) Trying to marry him for money, or C) Using them to do her dirty work.

A guy as a friend was a novelty.

Even though she really liked Jason and was already fantasizing about something more with him, she was terrified of losing just about the only friend she had...

But, boy was he gorgeous.

He wasn't too tall (unlike James who had made her feel like a shrimp) and had a congeniality that warmed her heart. She could feel him and God breaking down her barriers and defenses. She knew she could actually fall in love with this man. And not with any ulterior motives - for real.

He patted the sofa. "Come sit by me."

She got goose bumps and a speeding heartbeat. He looked at her closely as she sat down.

"And how are you today, Lorie?"

Truthfully, she liked when he called her that. It made her feel young - something she didn't think she'd ever felt.

Shyly, she said, "I'm fine."

"That - you are."

She giggled. "And how are you, Dr. Scott?"

He looked at her intently. His face eased in closer to hers and her heart began to race faster.

"I'm feeling better by the minute," he said huskily.

He reached around and undid the ponytail that she had gotten in a habit of wearing.

"I like your hair down - you know that. Just like when I first saw you awake." She flinched from the memory. "No, don't," he soothed. "Remember, I don't want you to feel bad about anything that's happened in the past. You're a brand new creature. You were beautiful that day. Don't forget it."

She trembled. He touched her bottom lip with his thumb and began caressing it.

"Remember the problem I said I still struggle with?" His voice was low and was doing things to her. She was melting into a big puddle.

"Yes," she said in a daze.

"My problem is that I still struggle with my flesh when it comes to a beautiful woman I want. And that beautiful woman is you."

He inched closer and his lips tentatively touched hers. She thought she would ignite. He eased in as if testing, tasting her lips. She trembled violently. She had never felt like this. Her heart was about to burst out of her chest.

He pulled her close and she froze a bit. She was anxious for so many reasons...

"Don't be afraid. I just want to hold you. I'm not going to hurt you, Lorie."

She allowed him to hold her and he gave fluttery kisses to her forehead, her cheeks, her closed eyelids, her nose and back to her lips. *She was really a baby that needed tender loving care*, he thought.

She had never felt such gentleness from a man.

"Lorie, open your eyes." She obeyed, looking at him in wonder. He smiled wide, his dimples on ten. "Can I kiss you?"

"Yes," she breathed.

His lips descended on hers. Giving gentle pecks as he continued where he left off - tasting her lips. Then his tongue was gently exploring her lips. He took her by the chin and tilted her mouth up to his, coaxing them apart. Once he had her mouth open and inviting, his tongue delved in with authority, tasting and seeking her tongue. She gave it to him and he savored and suckled it as if he needed it to live. He continued his feast for a long moment, coming back to nibble on her lips. He was driving her wild with passion. She was on fire. Nobody had *ever* kissed her like that. She felt something akin to butterflies exploding deep in the pit of her belly.

*What is this feeling?*

She put her arms up around his neck and pulled him in. She was so wound up that she leaned him over into the sofa, taking authority. Immediately, he gently pushed her back up. She let go in shame and put her head down in her hands.

"I'm sorry, I lost control. I'm such an idiot."

He gathered her into his arms, kissing her head.

"You're mistaken, that's not why I pulled away. The problem is that I loved every minute of it. Too much. And I knew if I didn't stop this, we'd be on our way upstairs."

She shivered at the thought.

"We have to exercise some control, but I knew the moment I let you live here, this could pose a problem."

"You were attracted to me back then?"

He smirked at her like she was nuts. "Since the day in the hospital. You didn't know?"

"No, you were laughing at me all of the time. I thought you thought I was ridiculous."

"I did," he admitted. "Ridiculous and funny and attractive," he said while giving her kisses to her forehead. "I couldn't stop thinking about you. Even after you were rude to me at the center, I couldn't get you off of my mind. I was just conjuring up an excuse to come back and see if you were still there when I received a call on my rental line," he laughed. "And I don't think it was by chance that it was you. After the things I've experienced, I believe in divine appointments," he said wistfully.

"I thought about you, too," she said shyly.

"You're joking. I thought you hated my guts."

She laughed. "I should've and I thought I did until I realized I wanted to prove to you how attractive I was after you saw me looking like a disaster in the hospital."

He chuckled and waved his finger. "You weren't a disaster at the hospital. You were a disaster at the center."

She swatted him and he tried to cover his face.

"Jason, you are much too honest! You need to consider a girl's feelings."

"I'm sorry. But don't you like it when I tell you the honest to goodness truth? You would still be walking around in all of that clown makeup if I didn't."

She punched him hard in the arm.

"Jason!"

He left shortly after, and she thought about him all night. Something was definitely happening between them. She felt like the naive teenager she had never gotten to be. She felt so vulnerable to finally admit to herself what she had been feeling for weeks...

She was falling in love.

# CHAPTER FOURTEEN

As promised, she called Justine from rehab. She picked up on the first ring.

"Hey, Girly, I was just thinking about you!"

"Really? When did you get out?"

"A few days ago. Did you find a place?"

"Yes, as a matter of fact I did."

Lorelei went on to explain how she accidentally ended up at Jason's apple orchard and that they were now dating.

"You're kidding me! That fine ass doctor that's a life coach from *Sunny Rivers*?"

She laughed at Justine's blunt reaction.

"Yes, that's him."

"Girl, that might be the best mistake you *ever* made."

Lorelei laughed along with Justine. She wondered if that was true...

§

The other car needed to go in for repairs and Jason knew Lorelei needed to go to the store the next day.

"Why don't you drop me off and use the car?"

"Are you sure you don't mind?"

"No, it's not a problem."

Once they arrived, he gave her a kiss and headed inside. Glancing down at the passenger seat, she realized he had forgotten his stethoscope. She guessed that he probably had another one inside the office, but she didn't want to take that chance.

She rushed in to find a pregnant woman in the waiting room looking a little flushed. Jason, who had just stepped behind the desk, turned around in surprise as he saw Lorie with the stethoscope.

He smiled warmly. "I actually don't have my other one here. It's at the hospital, thanks."

He pulled her into an examination room and shut the door. Thanking her properly, he lifted her up on the examination table and gave a long, thorough, two minute exploration of her mouth. Her arms went up around his neck of their own volition. He was easing in closer between her knees. Today, she had on a mini skirt. It was getting hot in here...

Just as he was about to grab her thighs to pull her closer, they heard the woman in the waiting room, wailing.

"Ooohh! I think my water broke while I was in the shower this morning and I'm in so much pain."

Jason rushed out towards the woman and Lorelei was behind him. She froze at the sight.

The lady had scooted forward out of her chair and was on the floor. Jason was kneeling down, feeling her abdomen.

"Why didn't you say anything earlier, Jeanette? How long have you been having contractions and how far apart?" he asked calmly.

"They've been happening for the last few hours...ugh...but now...they've gotten really bad! I...thought...the baby wouldn't be coming so soon - Aahhh!"

"Yeah, you aren't due for another two weeks. Okay, Lorie, I'm going to need your help. We don't have time to get to the hospital. This baby is coming now."

*What?*

At her stunned expression, he said calmly, "Rose is out sick today and Dr. Montague is at the hospital..." He looked around and at his watch, shaking his head, "maybe Rebecca is in the bathroom but we don't have time to waste." He looked at her pointedly. "So, you're going to help me deliver this baby. Now."

Lorelei was stunned. He was seriously asking for her help? He gave her a stern glare and she quickly snapped to it.

She helped Jason get the lady into a room that had a delivery table. She helped Jeanette get out of her maternity shorts and covered her up with a gown.

At this point, the woman was howling in distress.

"Easy, Jeanette. Take it easy. Lorie, help me place her legs in the stirrups."

Lorelei did everything The Good Dr. Scott requested.

She handed him all of the necessary tools and wiped Jeanette's forehead with a damp cloth.

Jason was in between Jeanette's raised legs, examining her.

"You're dilated ten centimeters. Don't push, Jeanette. Wait until I say so."

Jeanette grabbed onto Lorelei's hand, almost squeezing the life out of it. Lorelei was in pain but knew the other woman was in more. She continued to wail. Lorelei tried to calm her down by changing the subject.

"Where's your husband, Jeanette?"

That was a mistake. The woman started roaring loud, almost screaming.

"That fat bastard is out fishing with his buddies - I hate his guts!"

It took everything for Lorelei and Jason not to burst out laughing.

"Calm down, Jeanette. I can see the crown of the baby's head. On the count of three, I want you to push."

"Aahhh!"

"Wait, I haven't counted yet. One, two, three. Push."

"Aaarggh."

Lorelei hadn't been around such intensity in a while.

"Again. Push... almost here."

"Uuhhhhhh," Jeanette bellowed. Lorelei continued holding her hand and wiping her brow.

"Last one. Push!"

At that moment, Jason pulled out a slithery infant and held it up, smacking its bottom. The baby's plaintive cries filled the room. Jason suctioned the baby's mouth and nose with a small bulb syringe to remove any additional fluid.

"Congratulations, Jeanette, you have a healthy, handsome, baby boy."

Jeanette's agonized face broke into happy tears.

He placed the bloody baby on Jeanette's stomach after he cut the umbilical cord.

Lorelei was so overwhelmed at having to assist Jason. She had so many mixed emotions right now but the prevailing one was awe of his expertise as he single handedly delivered a baby. She was falling more in love with him every day. She knew she was forever changed by what she had just witnessed firsthand. She held back tears of joy.

"Good job, Lorelei. I'm glad you brought in my stethoscope." They both laughed.

This made her seriously consider nursing school.

Rebecca appeared in the doorway, sucking on a lollipop.

"What did I miss?"

§

Rebecca was fired and Jason convinced Lorelei to take over receptionist duty for a few days until they hired someone else. It was relatively easy since the phones didn't ring that much and it was nice to see Jason so frequently.

The other doctors and midwife were very nice to Lorelei, and she tried to help them out in any way possible. She was learning that it wasn't about Lorelei all of the time. She received immense gratification from helping someone else.

Occasionally, Jason would secretly give her his sultry, sexy smile, but Dr. Lillian was on to him.

"You can't fool me, I know you like that cute little thing right there."

Normally, Lorelei would've been livid at the term but she just giggled. Maybe being little and cute wasn't such a bad thing if Jason liked it…

He didn't deny it.

"That's right. I like that cute little thing and she likes me." He winked for affect.

Lorelei blushed harder than she thought possible.

Dr. Lillian covered her mouth in surprise as she laughed at his forwardness.

She nudged him.

"Oooh, you are so bad, Jason." She smiled at them both. "Finally." She patted his hand and walked away.

"What does that mean? *Finally*." Lorelei asked.

He smiled. "She and everyone else here have been trying to set me up on blind dates for years but I wouldn't budge. She can see that something special may be going on between us."

She smiled warmly, her insides in tingles. "Is it? Is something special going on?" she asked coyly.

He leaned in close over the reception desk and tilted her chin up to his.

"You tell me."

He gave her a resounding smooch on the lips, his eyes seductive but serious.

Just at the moment, Dr. Lillian came back around the corner, spotting their kiss.

"Get a room," she joked, walking past them into another exam room.

He smiled.

"Well, we have to do what the doctor says."

For the next few days while she was there, he frequently pulled her into empty exam rooms for impromptu make-out sessions. She was a willing patient.

She enjoyed her short-lived stint at his practice. It was fascinating to watch him in doctor mode. And it was such a turn on...

# CHAPTER FIFTEEN

They hired another receptionist named Amy, and later that week, they were back on her sofa after dinner. Deciding that they needed to take it easy, he left right after bible study. She admitted that reading the bible helped curb the strong feelings of desire. But whenever she saw him again, the desires were right back.

It must've been the same for Jason because the day after that, they skipped bible study and began making out on the sofa. They kissed like teenagers for hours.

Her arms were up around his shoulders and she was like a wild woman. She liked everything about Jason Scott. His smell, his chiseled face, his deep dimples, his strong arms and his spiky brown hair. Her mouth moved to the side and over to his ear, where she nibbled on his ear lobe and the area underneath.

He groaned loudly and the sound went to the very depths of her. She loved that she was able to evoke such primal sounds. Then she kissed her way down his neck, biting gently.

His moans got extremely loud and sensuous. He pulled her away, breathing fast.

"Lorie, we have to stop." No longer embarrassed about her passion, she tried to reach forward to continue kissing him. He grabbed her arms and placed her away from him, willing her to stop.

"Please, Lorie. Stop, listen to me," he said, rather forcefully.

That got her attention and she looked up at him with wide doe eyes as if she didn't see a problem.

He chuckled at her expression.

"You are so cute…and dangerous. Listen to me. I'm doing you a huge disservice here and I apologize."

"What are you talking about?"

"You are a newborn in Christ and I'm tempting you. You should be focused on the spiritual and I'm leading you into temptation. I forgot that you wouldn't know any better."

"There's nothing wrong with us kissing, is there?" she blinked innocently.

"No, but the way we're kissing tonight is definitely going to lead us to something else. At the office is one thing, but knowing there is a bed right around the corner is risky. I thought I could control it, but you're making me lose my mind."

"Oh." She was both flattered and frustrated.

"We're going to have to cool down from now on."

She pouted like a child. "I don't want to. I love kissing you."

He drew her back into his arms and planted a soft sensual peck on her lips. Just that little kiss was enough to incite her again. Automatically, she began deepening the kiss. He pulled away and placed his hands on both sides of her face to hold her still and look at her.

"See what I mean? We're too hot for each other." He stood up and started pacing, running his hands through his hair. "This is not good." He made his way towards the door, leaving her on the sofa, bewildered.

"Where are you going?" she asked in disappointment.

"I'm going home. Let's talk on the phone." He came back and gave her a resounding kiss on the lips before he left out the front door. She didn't feel too rejected because she knew he wanted her as much as she wanted him. She was just disappointed.

The next week, she and Jason didn't see each other as often as before. He came over a few times for bible study and dinner, but after a few chaste kisses, he left. She was reading more of the Bible, so she understood. And they were getting to know each other more from talking on the phone. Tonight, they were discussing their day but he soon grew quiet.

"What are you thinking about?" she asked.

"I'm thinking about you."

"What about me?"

"How beautiful you are to me and how much I want to be with you. How much I want you to be in my arms."

She melted at his words but had to admit she felt insecure about their relationship. She knew she was in love with him already, but knowing how terrible she had been as a person, deep down she felt she didn't deserve him.

Now she knew that it was the devil constantly bringing up her past. She was wise enough to know it was just the beginning. With everything she had done badly in her life, there would be reminders for years to come.

"What happened between you and Gina?"

He was silent for a moment, but knew if they were going to have a solid relationship; the subject of his ex-wife had to be broached.

"Gina and I were just from two separate worlds. She was never interested in…family…or God, so to speak. Not truly. We just…it just didn't work out." He knew he was giving her the edited version, but he wasn't in the mood to go into it.

"I'm sorry to hear that."

Truthfully, she couldn't be too mad at Gina. She had been like that once. After yearning for a family life she didn't have, she changed for the worse.

She was also insecure because her past fiancé's had other women.

"Jason, why are you single? You could have anyone you wanted."

"I told you that my colleagues have been trying to hook me up for years. No one has intrigued me in a long time."

She took a deep breath.

"In both of my past engagements, they had their own women."

He knew what she was getting at and was quiet as he thought about how she was feeling.

"I don't have any other women, if that's what you're wondering," he said carefully.

"I know you say that, but are you saying you've been abstinent since your ex-wife?"

He chuckled. "No, I'm not saying that. I'm human and I've slipped up more than enough times. It's always been a battle. I told you that."

Instead of helping, he could feel her closing up further. How could he reassure her?

"Lorie, I think you're beautiful and I'm very attracted to you. You're hilarious and I find you completely fascinating. Right now, I'm really grateful you've come into my life and I don't want to mess anything up. I think you're still hurting deeply… and you need to be healed. I want to help do that."

She warmed but was cautious.

"And what happens after I'm healed. Will you leave?" she asked in a small voice.

"Not if you want me to stay."

She was overjoyed by his response but he sensed she still had lingering doubts. He knew he was dealing with a deeply wounded soul.

"Look, Lorie. I can't convince you that I'm never going to stray. You're just going to have to take a leap of faith and trust me. Trust that the feelings I'm having are real. Trust that if things were to ever go further with us, not only would I not want to dishonor you, I wouldn't want to dishonor God. I'm more fearful of His chastening than anything else. That's why even though I stumble, I try to get myself back in line by immersing myself in His Word. That's the only thing that keeps me on the right path."

"Alright, I'll try."

He could sense that she was more at ease. "Good."

"When is Abby coming home?"

His voice brightened. "She'll be home in a few weeks for the rest of the summer. I can't wait for you to meet her."

Through the phone, she could tell that his eyes were shining from the mention of his baby girl…

After they hung up, she hugged her arms, terrified of how she was feeling. She felt she was on a precipice but was unsure about which direction she would fall. She wanted to head for the true happiness that was right in front of her - that she didn't know was possible for her. But she had some daunting decisions to make, and her life could go either way. If she and Jason were going to have a blessed, honest to God relationship, she had to let him know everything about her.

The problem was how would he react?

She got up and dug inside her drawer for a worn purple sachet that she'd kept for years. It was always stuck in the back of her drawer, no matter where she moved to. She hadn't looked inside of it in years. She gently pulled the frayed draw string and pulled out one of its contents. It was a tiny, pink chiffon flowered, silver gilded headband with a pink feather in the middle. She was too overwhelmed to pull out the other item. For the second time that month, Lorelei wept long and bitterly.

# TESTED

## PART V

### CHAPTER SIXTEEN

*Flashback: 1997*

Dutifully, Lorelei had been taking her studies very seriously at Clark Preparatory. Ever since her warning to the ridiculous heifers that thought they were going to punk her, she was left alone. The message had obviously made its way throughout the school. The looks she received were curious but cautiously blank. No doubt nobody wanted a knife up to the jugular like that trick, Amanda.

She didn't befriend a soul and that's just the way she wanted it. She hadn't been feeling that good anyway, kind of fatigued. And even though she wasn't eating that much, her clothes started fitting a little tighter. She chalked it up to too many sweets. *Better cut back...*

As summer vacation approached, she started feeling more bloated than ever. Along with that came a sense of dread. Concerned because her skirt was too tight, her nipples sore, and she had already missed a few periods, she went to the Planned Parenthood clinic not too far from her house. She'd never had regular periods anyway so she wasn't concerned at first, but the clothes were getting small fast.

A blood test revealed what she was in denial of for weeks. She was pregnant. The nurse smiled at her as she revealed the news. She looked at Lorelei for a response.

*What? Am I supposed to be ecstatic? I'm only sixteen, bitch.*

Not even thinking twice, Lorelei asked, "Where should I go to get rid of it?" The nurse was taken aback by her bluntness but quickly recomposed her features.

Lorelei wasn't stupid - she could see the chick was disappointed in her decision.

*Too bad - this is my body.*

"I'm sorry, you're past that stage," the nurse said with a hint of a satisfied smirk. "From what we can see, you're at least four or five months."

"What?" *Had it been that long?*

"And that isn't an option if you're past the first trimester and you are."

"Bull. I don't believe it."

This nurse patted her belly and Lorelei smacked her hand away. *The nerve of this ignorant…*

The nurse smiled in amusement.

"Well, since you couldn't tell us when your last period was, this is what we've determined. You have quite a bump growing there."

"Not good enough. Can I get an ultrasound or something?"

"Sure, but that's going to cost."

"Money is no object."

Sure enough, after the expensive ultrasound, it was determined that she was almost five months pregnant.

*Shit, the parents are going to hit the roof!*

§

Lorelei was devastated she didn't catch this in time. She knew it had to be that evil Jeff Mays that knocked her up. In turn, she hated the situation and the baby that was sucking the life out of her. This was ruining all of her plans.

She waited until school was out for the summer before she broke the news to her parents. They had been excited about arrangements they were making to move to Chicago to open a huge manufacturing plant. It would be three times the size of the one here and would push them over into the status of running with the big dogs. This opportunity would help them with their goal to expand to other big cities and eventually go global.

They were so over the moon, they didn't notice that their only daughter was blowing up like a big fat balloon. They probably wouldn't pay attention until she actually handed over the baby.

It was the weekend and they were at the kitchen table with blueprints and papers everywhere, strategizing for the Chicago plant.

"Ed, Mallory, I need to talk to you."

"Not now, we're busy. Can't you see we're busy?" her mother dismissed.

"But I really need to talk to you guys."

Mallory pounded the table. "Dammit, what is it now?"

Her father never stopped looking at the blueprints or furiously writing.

She knew she would have to beg.

"Please, something has happened and I really need to talk to you."

121

For the first time in months, both of her parents turned to look at her. *Really*, look at her. By this time, there was no hiding the baby bump. She had been successful at school, but even if somebody suspected, they wouldn't dare have the balls to say anything. She had been wearing oversized sweaters for the last few months. Thank goodness she was so small. She believed she had gotten away with it. Now, she was too far gone.

Her mother took one look at her stomach and fell over onto the floor, holding her chest and hyperventilating.

"Oh my god, what has this tramp done?"

Ed immediately went down to the floor to help his wife up.

"Easy Mal, easy Mal." Her mother was still screeching and wailing as he helped her up.

Typical Ed, always the last to know, was ignorant of what was transpiring.

"What have you done, Lorie? What's wrong with your stomach?"

Mallory immediately stopped wailing and punched him in the arm.

"What do you think, ya big dope? She's knocked up!"

Then she immediately continued wailing like a complete psycho. Lorelei calmly went to sit down on the sofa. This was the reaction she was expecting and she wasn't surprised. Truthfully, it was nice to finally have some attention - by any means.

After a few minutes, Mallory was able to get up. She marched over and slapped Lorelei hard across the face. She expected that, too.

"You friggin' slut! I knew you would do it. You're out to ruin this family! Why do you hate us so much? We're trying our best for you and this family. Why didn't you get rid of it?"

The words cut Lorelei but she was geared up for her mother's vitriol. She wouldn't be Mallory if she didn't verbally abuse her like this. She knew she was going to continue to pound her with vicious words, so she said nothing.

"How could you do this to us? Why, why, why? I told you, Ed, I should've gotten rid of *her*. Then we wouldn't' be going through this!"

Lorelei flinched at her words. Her mother had wanted to get rid of her? That was unexpected. If she wasn't feeling worthless already, she surely did now.

Ed did nothing but try to comfort his wife who started wailing again.

"Mal, that's too harsh now. Cut it out and calm down." Then he turned like a cobra on Lorelei. "But really, Lorie, how could you do this to us? We're just about to have all of our dreams come true. How did you get yourself into this situation? Why weren't you being safe?"

She was cold to the bone after her mother's chilling revelation. Numb, she tried to speak, but nothing would come out.

"Tell me!" her father demanded. She hadn't seen him this angry since the incident in fourth grade.

After a few moments, she was able to speak.

"It was a mistake. I'm sorry. I just found out a month ago but by that time, it was too late." Her voice quivered and she began to cry. This woke her mother up from wailing.

"Oh, you've got to be kidding me, trifling tramp!" She got up and smacked Lorelei once more across the face. That one would definitely leave a bruise. Then she pointed at her sniffling daughter. "You have no right to cry! You did this to yourself and us. I don't want to hear it!"

Lorelei slid to the floor and began to howl loudly. Ed was still comforting his wife. Lorelei knew he would never comfort her. She was always last priority - or not at all.

"Mal, you can't keep hitting her like that. She's preg..."

She rounded on him.

"Why not, we're not keeping that unborn bastard. She is NOT keeping it! It'll ruin our reputation. What will everyone say?"

He shook his head in dismay while Mallory continued her rant.

"Oh my god - and she's enrolled at Clark Prep!" She focused her attention back to Lorelei. "Listen, tramp, does anyone know about this?" Her eyes were livid as if she was going to smack Lorelei if she gave the wrong answer.

"No. No one," Lorelei hiccupped.

"How did you keep it hidden at school?"

"I didn't really start showing until recently and I was covered up," she whined. "Nobody would've said anything anyway," she had the nerve to say smugly.

Mallory jabbed her finger into the middle of Lorelei's chest. "You better hope no one knows anything. If word gets back to us that the cat is out of the bag, I will personally strangle you, you no good tramp."

§

Lorelei wasn't allowed out of the house for a week. At the end of the next week, at 4:30 in the morning, she was smuggled out of the house into a cab for a two hour drive to upstate New York. It was a maternity home for women with unplanned pregnancies. She was to give the baby up for adoption as soon as it was born.

The place was a dormitory type residence that was private and out in the middle of nowhere. For the next three months, she kept to herself. She read a lot and watched television, of course. Her belly grew and the baby was constantly kicking around inside of her as if it knew Lorelei's intentions.

*Yeah, I don't like you, either.*

Otherwise, she was numb just thinking about her mother's revelation and the mess that she had gotten herself into. She didn't want this child, no matter what. *Jeff Mays' child? Ugh.* Truthfully, it could've been one of the other guys she messed around with, but blaming it on him just felt right. She knew the "withdrawal method" wasn't exactly a safe guarantee. She tried not to think about it too much.

The director, Jacqueline Cooley, was a no-nonsense, but compassionate woman. Lorelei had assured her that she wasn't interested in being involved in placing the child for an open adoption, such as choosing parents and so forth. She just wanted to be rid of it so she could get on with her life.

One day in her seventh month, she went to her regularly scheduled ultrasound. There was a new technician she hadn't seen before. She wondered where the regular tech was.

"Hi, I'm Natalie. I'm new and I'll be taking over for Sandra who is on vacation.

Lorelei shrugged.

Once she started examining the baby through ultrasound, Lorelei got into her routine position which was to face away from the screen. She had no interest.

"Oh, look at her. She's healthy and strong." Lorelei jerked her head around towards Natalie.

Natalie dropped the wand and put her hand over her mouth.

"Oh my god, I'm so sorry! I keep forgetting that I'm not supposed to say anything like that here." Lorelei just looked at her in shock, and then her eyes riveted to the screen.

She was having…a baby girl?

Meanwhile, Natalie continued rambling, "I'm so sorry. Please don't' say anything or I'll be fired. I really need this job. My last job was in a regular hospital where patients didn't mind knowing…"

But Lorelei was transfixed. She could see the perfect image of a perfect baby.

*Her* baby girl.

§

126

Lorelei was devastated and forever damaged by Natalie's slip up. She realized that the little life growing inside of her was a real, actual person. A girl.

On a weekly trip off the grounds, the bus took them into town where the expectant mothers could do some light shopping for personal needs. Lorelei needed some more sneakers - her swollen ankles and feet were killing her. Looking in the shoe aisle at Wal-Mart, her eyes were drawn to the next aisle over - baby stuff. Like an automaton, she was drawn over towards the baby accessories. Her eyes fell on a tiny pink chiffon flowered, silver gilded headband. Right in the middle was a pink feather. It was precious. Precious like the life inside her. She was overwhelmed with something she had never felt before…

Intense love.

After that, she watched all of the ultrasounds and even requested a scan. Director Cooley was informed about Lorelei's new interest in the child.

"Ms. Sampson, I was told that you seem to be growing attached to the child. Are you still willing to place the child up for adoption?"

She swallowed her tears. She had been crying so much lately. She knew that time with her daughter was winding down. Mallory would never let her live it down if she went against her wishes. Plus, what was she going to do with a baby anyway? Someone else could love the child better than her, she reasoned.

*Give her a good home with real parents - not those cold, unfeeling vultures I live with.*

"Yes, I haven't changed my mind."

The director hesitated. "Are you sure? You know you don't have to do this if you aren't sure. There are lots of programs that can assist you if you change your mind-"

"No," she said, gulping, "I'm not going to change my mind."

§

In September, Lorelei gave birth to a seven pound baby girl. The doctors performed a C-section since Lorelei was so tiny. She never saw her baby as it was whisked out of the room while a large divider was over her chest. She cried and grabbed a nurse.

"Please tell them when they do the birth certificate I have a name for the child."

The nurse gently pried Lorelei's hand away from her arm and patted her hand soothingly.

"You need to rest, dear…"

"No!" Lorelei said vehemently, taking the nurse by surprise. "I have a name for my daughter."

§

Afterwards, Lorelei was taken back to her room to rest and cried for hours. She did everything in her power to keep from running through the halls towards the nursery to find her daughter. She had never felt such pain and it wasn't from giving birth.

Director Cooley came to visit her with the forms to relinquish her rights, again grilling her on whether she had changed her mind. She needed her to be sure because there were foster parents lined up that wanted to adopt her child right away. Lorelei was in agony. She didn't know she was capable of feeling such loss. She had weighed the decision over and over in her mind.

*This might be the only person that loves me.*

But then she thought about her future and knew she was too selfish.

"Yes, I'm sure." A lone tear escaped. "But before signing away my rights, can I name my baby girl?"

Not surprised that she knew the sex, the director nodded. Expectant mothers always had the option to know the sex of the baby, whether it was an open adoption or not, but most mothers who did not want an open adoption chose not to.

"Of course you can. Just know that there is the possibility that the adopted parents could change the child's name, but on the original certificate will be you and the name you choose."

Lorelei had some semblance of peace with that revelation.

*The least I can do is name my baby girl…*

"Her name is Abigail. Abigail Sampson."

*-End of Flashback-*

# CHAPTER SEVENTEEN

After a few hours of weeping, she slowly returned the purple sachet and its contents back to the drawer. She knew she would have to tell Jason the truth. She had to consider this if their relationship was to continue. Who's to say he wouldn't want another child? They were both still young enough. She knew she was jumping the gun, but these were things she had to consider. Plus, he obviously loved children since he delivered babies.

The next day, she was up on a ladder picking apples when she saw Jason drive up from work. He went to the mailbox and headed back into the house with a large envelope. As he glanced at it, his mouth was set in a grim line and he had a look of trepidation that she wouldn't forget. Noticing her presence, he waved to her before disappearing inside.

*What was that about?*

She didn't see him for days after that.

§

He remembered a conversation he'd had on the phone with Abby a few weeks ago. They had been laughing about something funny that had happened to her and a friend at school. He also mentioned to her that there was a new tenant staying in the coach house and that they were dating. She wasn't happy, but she never was when it came to women around her dad. Sometimes she acted like he was her boyfriend.

"Ugh, so have you kissed her?"

"That's none of your business, young lady."

"Eww, that means yes. What's this one like?"

"You act like I have a new lady friend every day."

She laughed, "No, you haven't been bringing anyone around for months now."

"More than months - years. I haven't seriously dated since you were about twelve. Be fair."

"Okay, you're right. I'm just kidding, Dad."

"And I hope you're more mature than you were back then. You always caused them so much grief."

"That's because I could tell they weren't any good. You'd been hurt before and I didn't want to see that again. I have to look after you, you know."

His heart warmed at her over protectiveness. It was usually just he and Abby against the world.

She was quiet for a moment.

"Abby, you still there?"

"Yeah." She was silent and he knew she had something on her mind. "Dad...?" she began apprehensively.

"What is it?"

"I think...I want to know."

He knew what she was talking about. They had talked about it years ago after Gina left, but he knew it had never completely left her mind. It had never left either of their minds.

"Are you sure?" he asked cautiously.

"Yes, I really want to know," she said softly.

131

He sighed inwardly.

"Alright," he said, slapping the table resolutely.

§

Today, he walked inside and sat down at the kitchen table again, exhausted and bit anxious. He knew Lorie was probably wondering why he didn't linger and make small talk when he drove up, but this was way too pressing. He would see her later...

In his possession was an envelope that contained the results of his inquiry. It had taken a few exhaustive weeks for his buddy Mark, a private detective, to find what he was looking for. The first mistake was having Mark search through the boroughs of New York. That was the first roadblock. Then he told him to try New York State. He needed Mark to use his resources and expertise since Jason wasn't on the original birth certificate. There were procedures established by the State.

Eventually, Mark was able to obtain non-identifying information from the agency Abby came to him through. He traced it back to the first foster parents in an adoption that supposedly never happened. That led to the place of birth, Warren, New York, which was upstate. They had finally found the actual agency that arranged the first foster care. Mark was subsequently able to get the final documentation.

He used the letter opener to make a smooth slit at the top of the envelope and pulled out the official document.

It was the original birth certificate of his daughter.

It read:

Certified Certificate of Birth, State of New York Department of Health

Date of Birth: September 4, 1997

Date Filed: September 5, 1997

Name: Abigail Sampson

He stopped cold when his eyes moved down to the next line.

Mother's Maiden Name: Lorelei Sampson

Breaking out into a cold sweat, he thought his heart would stop.

# CHAPTER EIGHTEEN

Lorelei hadn't heard from Jason in two days. She tried calling him but it went straight to voicemail. Remembering his face and how serious he had looked that day, she decided to venture over to knock on his door. She saw the SUV in the driveway so she knew he had to be home. He didn't come to the door.

Now, completely bewildered, she went back to the house and waited. She was getting more into the Bible and utilizing it for peace. Ever since she had taken out the purple sachet, she had been in turmoil.

She studied and recited, Philippians 4:6 which said, *Be anxious for nothing, but by prayer and supplication with thanksgiving, make your requests known to God and the peace of God that passes all understanding, shall guard your hearts and minds through Christ Jesus.* Amazingly, it worked.

She had also made a decision that whenever he came over, she would tell him about the baby.

She began to pray.

"Dear Lord, please give me the strength to cast all of my burdens on you as you said in your Word. And please let Jason be okay - give him peace and strength, whatever he is going through. Thank you, In Jesus' Name, Amen."

Later the next day, there was a knock on the door. It was Jason.

He looked solemn and like he hadn't slept for days. She hurriedly let him into the house.

He was gazing at her peculiarly, but she ignored it. For the first time, she was actually more concerned about him than what he was thinking of her.

"Are you okay? What's wrong?"

He didn't answer but ran his hands through his hair and made his way to the sofa - the large sofa.

Taking the hint, she sat down, but further away than usual. At this point, she couldn't help but be concerned that his absence had something to do with her.

Had she done something wrong? Had he seen the tape?

He still hadn't uttered a word and it had been over two days. Amazingly, she still had peace.

"Jason, tell me. What's wrong? Did I do something wrong?"

He rolled his eyes up in his head and chuckled without humor.

He turned to her directly.

"I have some things I need to tell you. A lot of things, actually."

Was he breaking up with her? Now was probably a good time to confess her secret.

She bravely faced him on the sofa and got situated.

"Well, first, I have something to tell you."

His eyebrows shot up in surprise.

"Okay," he said slowly.

"Jason, I'm trying to be honest with you about everything that's happened in my past. There was something I left out when I told you my story."

He nodded. "Go on."

"Okay." She took a deep breath. "When I was sixteen, I gave birth to a child."

His eyes looked at her incredulously, but not for the reason she thought. He was shocked she was confessing it to him - first.

"I know. I'm sorry I didn't tell you but I was too ashamed. I could say that my mother made me give up the baby for adoption, but that would be a half-truth. I could've fought to keep the baby, but I didn't. I was…violated… by someone. That was one of the reasons why I didn't want to keep it…at first." She shook her head. "The truth is…I'm not even sure *he* was the father. I'm so ashamed." She buried her head in her hands.

He had mixed emotions about her confession.

"It was the biggest mistake of my life. I was too selfish, so I let the baby go," she confessed sadly, "but not before I found out that it was a girl." Her eyes grew wistful. "Her name was Abigail." Lip quivering, her eyes teared up as she said her name.

He said nothing for a long moment. He was looking at her in astonishment, shaking his head.

Again, she assumed wrong.

"So, I can understand if this news is too much for you," she rambled, "but I thought you should know, if…if…we were going to continue to see each other."

He shook his head slowly. "Lorelei, look - it's not anything like that. I'm not even upset at you right now. I'm in a state of shock. I've been in the state of shock for the last few days."

"Why?"

Leaning back, he rolled his eyes again and chuckled up towards the ceiling. He let out a long sigh.

She was getting impatient. "What is it, Jason. Just tell me," she pleaded.

He sat back up and turned towards her. "Okay, but I want you to be prepared, because it has to do with what you just told me."

"What is it?" she insisted, not even imagining how there could be a connection.

"I'm... happy that you told me about the...your child that you had at sixteen." He took a deep breath. "I found the baby."

Her mouth and eyes opened wide in shock, totally disbelieving what she was hearing. Her heart began to race so fast, she thought she would faint.

Finally she was able to speak. "What...what...are you talking about?" she asked quietly.

He handed her a document she hadn't noticed he'd had.

She read the certificate, covered her mouth and began to weep. She was trembling violently, the paper shaking in her other hand. He looked on in amazement.

"How...how...how did you get this?"

"Lorelei, you need to get yourself together, because this is just the beginning."

She tried to gather herself but she was both overjoyed and frightened - more than she had ever been. She was still trembling as he continued.

"I wasn't looking for her for you. I had no idea that you had anything to do with it. Abby...Abigail. Abigail is my daughter."

She stopped crying and opened her eyes and mouth in complete astonishment. She hadn't even put the names together. He thought she was going to have a seizure because she remained in that state for over a minute. Then she started trembling violently again. He knew this was too much for her. It was too much for him, and that's why he had to stay away. He knew he had to intervene before she passed out.

"Come here, Lorie."

"No," she wailed. "I can't. I can't....I don't understand...I can't..." Kicking into doctor mode, he was concerned she was about to become catatonic.

He held on to her forearms, trying to calm her down.

"I don't understand..." she wailed, shaking her head.

"Calm down and I'll explain."

He explained that a few weeks ago, Abby requested that he search for her mother. She had been considering it for years and he had told her that if she was ever curious, he would do it. He explained how it had been a wild goose chase, but they were finally able to find the original birth certificate.

"Had you ever thought about searching for her yourself?" he asked.

She swallowed hard and a fresh stream of tears followed.

"Truthfully, no. Of course I've thought about her over the years, wondering what she looked like, how old she would be...," she squeezed her eyes closed, tightly, "but those thoughts were extremely painful... and....I tried to block them out with substances and focusing on material things. I came away from that experience more bitter than ever."

She broke down again and he waited patiently until she composed herself.

"I felt I had just deprived myself of the one person who might've ever loved me. After that, I had nothing left to lose. So in turn, I didn't care whose back I stomped over to obtain the status and wealth that I thought would help cover the pain. It didn't work. And I felt she was better off not having a lunatic for a mother, anyway. I never told anyone of my true feelings because I was too ashamed…"

She started sobbing again and he took her into his arms and allowed her to cry. After a few minutes, she pulled away quickly, grabbing his arms in desperation and searching his eyes.

"What's she like? Can I see a picture? Please - these are things I've always wondered about. "

"Yes. And there will be plenty of time for you to see her. Since this is her request, she wants to meet you, too. There is a problem though. I haven't actually told her what I've found or that you're her mother. She knows that I have a tenant I'm dating - but I haven't told her the connection. I feel like that's something we should tell her together."

Lorelei shook her head in amazement, still trying to grasp what was happening.

"I can't believe that she's with you. What are the chances that this could have happened like this?" Then it hit her. "Wait, I thought Gina was her mother."

"Gina and I got married when Abby was six and we divorced a little over a year later. I was just starting medical school and really wanted Abby to have a mother figure, especially since school was stressing me out and I had started drinking. Gina pretended she was ready to step up to the plate. I realized later she had no intention of being a real mother to Abby. She thought that along with the status of being a future doctor's wife would come the perks of high society. You know, like 'ladies who lunch' and all that?"

She nodded. Lorelei knew full well what that meant. That life seemed a million miles away from her now…

"Once she realized I needed actual help with my daughter and saw that I intended for my practice to be out here in the country, she realized she'd hooked the wrong doctor-to-be. She was a big city girl who had her eyes on my wallet. I knew that, but fell for her anyway. Then, when I gave up alcohol by drawing closer in my walk with God, she wanted no parts of it. That's when I knew it wasn't going to work out. Abby was going on eight when we split up. I knew that all of the drama with the divorce proceedings affected her, but I don't think she ever felt any maternal connection with Gina."

She nodded in understanding.

"After we split up, Abby became super protective concerning any woman I dated. She and her friend, Candice used to play pranks on the women to scare them off."

Lorelei had no choice but to laugh at that one.

"She sounds like a chip off the old block," she said, remembering her bullying days.

"She's that. Listen," he said, turning towards her. "When I met you, I kept looking at you. Not only were you familiar to me, but you reminded me of someone. I didn't tell you that. That day on the beach when you had your eyes closed, that was when I really could see it but it didn't click until now. It was Abby. You reminded me of her when you were relaxed."

She was amazed at his words and frantic to see a picture of her. Sensing that she couldn't wait another moment, he pulled up a picture on his phone.

Lorelei looked at the young girl that looked like her. She had a cherubic, round face like she had when she was younger, but Lorelei thought she was much prettier. She had long, brownish red hair and intelligent, almond-shaped eyes, except they were blue like hers. She had deep dimples. She was beautiful. Lorelei began to weep for the daughter she had never seen but always imagined.

"Oh my god, she's beautiful, Jason. This is all too overwhelming for me. I can't believe….this is so amazing….I don't know what to do."

"Just let it sink in. We have a few weeks before she comes home, so…just relax, if you can. There's more from where that came from."

"What do you mean?"

"Remember I said I had a lot to tell you? It's not over yet."

# CHAPTER NINETEEN

*Flashback: 1999*

In August, Derrick finished packing up he and Little Gail's belongings and they boarded a midnight train to Georgia.

Hey, it was cheaper.

He had some fond memories of New York but knew they needed a change of scenery and a fresh start. There weren't any relatives left up here from his mother's side. He didn't know his father's folks so he didn't mind leaving. Hell, he didn't know his father. He had tried to contact him with the number his mother had left to alert him of her passing, but just like her constant voice messages to him, they went unreturned.

He knew there was more family down south than in New York and that would be good for Little Gail.

Gail loved looking out the window on the train. She sat on his lap with her face pressed to the window of the Amtrak.

"Daddy, fast. We go fast."

She would be two next month and her vocabulary was expanding every day.

They arrived in Savannah where his mother's brother, Martin was waiting.

"I'm glad you two made it safely."

"Thanks, Uncle Marty."

Uncle Marty was in his sixties and had a huge potbelly that Gail obviously remembered from when he was in town for his mother's services. Gail flew down from his arms and went right into Uncle Marty's arms.

"Hey, she has good taste," he said, smiling delightedly. He gave Little Gail a kiss on the cheek as they got into Marty's car to head to the country.

Uncle Marty owned a farm and coerced him to come down so he could give him a hand. He also thought it would be a good change for Little Gail. They immediately moved into the house with his uncle.

Uncle Marty insisted that Derrick not give up on school because of circumstances and a new daughter. He had explained to Uncle Marty about the crazy revelation that she was actually his biological daughter. Uncle Marty was amazed but felt it was an act of God. He went to church often with Marty and his great Aunt Susie. Marty and Susie took turns taking care of Gail while he prepared for school.

Before he had left New York, he reached out to his father one last time, but with no response. The jerk was never man enough to marry his mother, Barbara West, in the first place and was never a father to begin with. But she had given Derrick his surname and had always called him by his father's first name. He recalled a conversation he'd had with his mother.

"Mom, why do you call me that?

"Because you're so much like your father."

"I hope not, he's nowhere around."

He had forgiven his father, but didn't respect the way he never stepped up to the plate like Derrick had to with Little

Gail - and he was just eighteen! Therefore, wiping the slate clean, he enrolled at the University of Savannah and went by his first name...

Jason.

Jason Derrick Scott.

*-End of Flashback-*

# TRIED

## PART VI

### CHAPTER TWENTY

Lorelei was absolutely blown away when he finished his story. He told her about his mother bringing the child home, the accident, his mother's passing, his suspicions about Abby and the subsequent DNA test. She tried to grasp what he was saying.

She could not believe her ears.

The first whopper was that he had found her daughter.

Next, that her daughter was *his* Abby. She had automatically assumed he had adopted her when he revealed the birth certificate.

And the kicker – Jason was actually Abby's biological father and Lorelei was the biological mother. It wasn't making much sense to her and she needed clarification.

"What are you saying?"

"Lorelei. You and I obviously messed around in high school. I vaguely remember that, but…it happened. You gave birth to our child. That child was brought home by my mother and then I found out the child was actually my biological daughter."

Her head was spinning. She shook her head, trying to gain some semblance of reality.

"That sounds preposterous."

"I thought so too. But like I said before, I believe in divine appointments. Nothing should really surprise me now. This whole thing with Abby started my belief in a higher power. What would be the chances?"

"I always thought...I was so sure that it was Jeff Mays... the guy who..."

"The guy who raped you?"

She cringed at his words. "I wouldn't call it that exactly. I was so bad back then..."

He shook her arms. "Did he take you against your will?"

"Yes, but..."

"Then that's what it was. The act is not to be excused because of how you behaved back then. It's good that you've forgiven him and moved on, but don't minimize what he did."

"Alright."

"From what I can remember, you didn't want much to do with me after we got together. I let it go, moved on to someone else and you disappeared. I don't remember seeing you anymore and honestly, I didn't think about you anymore."

"I transferred to a private school before I started to show. I did disappear."

He nodded in understanding.

"Okay, that makes sense. When I found out that Abby was mine, I tried to remember the girls I had been with that year. It was so hard because there had been about four or five. I had it narrowed down to two girls. One of them was you but I still couldn't be sure. It was only when I saw you again and remembered that you and I might have dated that the possibility struck me but I brushed it away. Then I kept thinking you reminded me of someone, and like an idiot, I couldn't see that it was my own daughter until after I got the birth certificate. For the past few days, I've been trying my best to recollect our time together but everything is so hazy."

Once again, she was totally flabbergasted by what he was saying.

She wracked her brain trying to remember him.

"I don't remember a Jason before I left.... Wait a minute. You went by...Derrick, right?"

He nodded.

Again, she studied his features closely and tried to remember a sixteen year old *Derrick*. Something in her mind clicked.

"I think I remember now. You were a guy that wanted me to go out with you, but on our date we went all the way, right there on the spot." She grabbed her head in shame. "I think I remembered that you smelled good, like you do now. It was our first and only date. I was so awful."

"Well, I was a young teenaged guy back then, too - and I took what I could get. So it's not only your fault."

Tears began to well up in her eyes again. She couldn't remember ever feeling so mortified - and in front of the man she loved. A man who happened to be a guy she'd had a child with and didn't even know it. She felt the lowest of the low.

Reading her expression, he said, "Hey, it is what it is. Let's look at the reward. Abby."

She gave him a watery smile once he said her name.

"Why did you go from calling her Little Gail to Abby?"

"On the adoption papers my mother was to file, I saw that her first name was really Abigail. When she was three, I made sure she knew it and how to write it for school. She got to the first grade and thought Little Gail sounded country and started demanding that I call her Abby." He laughed at the memory. "Apparently, there was some other girl in her school named Abigail and that's what everyone called her. So, I went along with it and she's been *Abby* ever since."

"You said her name was to be Abigail West on the adoption papers your mother had filled out?"

"Yes. Once I found out that she was my biological daughter, I had her name officially changed from Abigail Jones, which was the name she came to us with, to Abigail Scott. Turns out, since the test proved she was mine, I didn't have to adopt her. Jones was the previous foster parent's names and I don't know how they were able to officially give her their last name for an adoption that supposedly never went through. It was a mess."

Lorelei immediately thought of her time at the facility and the compassionate and competent Director Cooley. Her eyes glazed over in remembrance.

"I remember that the foster parents were ready and waiting to adopt Abigail. Everything seemed to be set up precisely. At least, that's what the director told me and I sensed that she was very efficient. I wonder what happened that it didn't go through." Her eyes lit up. "Maybe it did go through. Maybe there was a tragedy of some sort and that led Abigail to your mom. For some reason, maybe Abigail had to go back into the system."

He had never thought of that. He looked at her in amazement that she could actually shed some light on a question that had dogged him for years. That's right, she was Abby's mother. She had been there. He was stunned at this huge revelation and how everything had turned out like it had.

"That never occurred to me. I never knew Abby's original last name and my mom didn't have those papers. At the time, I couldn't get an original birth certificate because I wasn't on it."

"What a mess I caused. If only I had kept her, maybe I could've eventually found out that you were..."

"Stop it, Lorelei. It's useless to talk about what you should've done differently. It's already done. We're here. We've all found our way back. God was always in control."

She nodded, in awe of how everything worked out. Her eyes flooded.

"This is unbelievable and so... awesome, this has to be an act of God," she said, smiling through tears.

"Absolutely. It has to be and it is."

He smiled wistfully.

"A door was closed when my mother passed away so suddenly like that. But God, in His infinite wisdom, opened another one and brought me Abby, my own daughter out of nowhere. How incredible is that? And she helped heal my broken heart."

Lorelei smiled, loving the way he looked at everything.

"Since my mom was so crazy about Abby, I gave her my mom's name. Abigail Barbara West Scott."

"That was nice. So we all had some part in naming her."

§

Jason and Lorelei were so overwhelmed by the bombshells that had dropped. On the sofa, they held each other tight for hours. They were quietly thinking about everything that had transpired and what would happen next. They were both shell shocked and overloaded with information.

"What happened to Uncle Marty?"

"Uncle Marty is in his seventies and after Aunt Susie passed, he remarried and relocated to his wife's hometown in Tennessee," he said smiling. "He calls and checks up on us from time to time."

"You didn't mind that he left the orchard to you?"

"No. I wanted it. As long as I had some help, I didn't see it as a problem. Abby loved it while she was growing up and it means a lot to us. We have some happy memories down here."

"That's good. This is a beautiful place."

He hugged her tightly.

She held her breath and then asked, "How do you feel about everything? How do you feel about me, now, Jason?"

He hugged her tightly in reassurance. "What do you mean?"

"I feel like I've just come into your life with all of these crazy revelations that could turn you off from me. In all honesty, I can understand how your ex-wife Gina felt because I was like that once. Money hungry and ambitious for wealth and status. Are you worried that I have ulterior motives?"

"No, because I don't make enough money for the old Lorelei," he laughed. "So I know you like me for me. I also know you're a changed woman. My spirit says so. I know you're for real. Now if we had met a few years ago, I don't know..." he trailed off.

Reassured, she laughed but grew serious again.

"I'm glad you feel that way, but I'm also concerned that you might think I'm staking some claim to your daughter."

"She's your daughter, too." Lorelei looked doubtful and he patted her shoulder in reassurance." I know, I know. I know what you really mean."

"She's my biological daughter - but I'm not her mom. Not...yet?" She said sadly but with hope.

"Do you want to be? Are you prepared to be a mom to her? Because that's why I think she wanted me to search for you."

Lorelei searched deep inside of her feelings to determine the answer. In truth, she was terrified.

"I do. I'm just scared she won't accept me. And I feel she shouldn't accept me, either. Not with the way I was and the way I let her go. I don't deserve anything remotely resembling love from her."

He squeezed her. "Shush, that's not true. Aren't you a new creature in Christ? Well, Jesus died to restore everything back to its natural order. Of course He would want you reconciled to your child if that's what you desire and that's what she desires."

She hadn't looked at it that way.

"What if she hates me?"

He chuckled. "Hate is too strong of a word and she wasn't raised to hate. Now, there is a distinct possibility that she might dislike you, but in time, things can change."

"I deserve whatever I'm going to get from her. I abandoned her."

"In time, she may understand. We just have to explain everything to her - what happened with Jeff and your reasons, etc. She may not be as unreasonable as you think."

# CHAPTER TWENTY ONE

Abby came home two weeks later. Jason and Lorie spent time reading the Bible and praying for understanding and direction. Their romance had taken a bit of a back seat to the huge development that was before them.

They went from romantically making out like teenagers to joint biological parents of a fifteen year old, overnight. Although they prayed for peace, it was a battle to keep from losing out to anxiety.

Lorelei was at home dusting and rearranging pillows for the millionth time when there was a knock on the door. She knew it was Jason who had gone to pick up Abby from the train station in downtown Sheridan.

She opened the door to Jason and a breathtakingly beautiful, Abby. Pictures did not do her justice. She was about five foot three and slender, had light chestnut hair down to her waist and strikingly beautiful, blue eyes. She could see that despite their blue color, Abby had Jason's almond shaped eyes and his hint of dimples, even though she wasn't smiling. She could see herself in Abby too. She obviously inherited Lorelei's eye color, petite frame and hair color.

Lorelei tried to gather her resolve and continued to pray for strength. This was actually her daughter. *Her* daughter. She held tightly onto the door knob to keep her knees from buckling. The young girl glared at her as Lorelei stared back in awe. She quickly tried to gather her wits and received a peace.

"Please, come in."

"Lorelei, this is my daughter, Abigail. Abby, this is my friend, Lorelei. I call her Lorie."

She heard the waver in Jason's voice. He was trying to keep his composure as well.

"Hi, Abby."

Without speaking or looking directly at Lorelei, Abby came in and looked over the house, her blue eyes scrutinizing.

Jason was incredulous. "Abigail Scott, where are your manners?"

She rolled her eyes and continued looking around.

"Hi," she said with a dismissive wave. Then she abruptly turned to Lorelei. "Have you been rearranging things in here? This is not your house, you're only temporary."

Jason nudged Abby hard. "Abby," he warned.

Abby placed her hands on her hips. "Dad, isn't this the same lady we found floating up the river?"

Lorelei chuckled. "Yes, that's me. I heard you screamed loudly. Without that, you may not have gotten the attention of your dad to rescue me. So, for what it's worth, thank you," Lorelei, said casually.

Flummoxed, Abigail obviously wasn't ready for Lorelei's comeback. She crossed her arms.

"Dad, who *is* this lady?"

"That's enough, Abby. You're not too old for me to turn you across my knee - so you'd better watch your mouth."

Chastened, Abigail looked down and pouted. Lorelei suppressed a giggle.

"That's okay, Jason. She's territorial. Let her do her thing," Lorelei said, smoothly.

Abigail stopped and really looked at Lorelei for the first time.

"That's correct. I know you're dating my father - so I'm checking you out."

Lorelei laughed at the girl's audaciousness. She reminded Lorelei of herself so much at that age. She couldn't help the thrill of pride that went through her. DNA was amazing!

"I understand. Check me out. You have every right."

Jason chuckled at his two girls. He knew that between the two of them, atoms and cells in the universe were exploding. These two together were a force to be reckoned with. He knew that his daughter had never met anyone like Lorelei before. She would be thrown off her axis. And possibly - vice versa.

Not sure how to respond, Abby smiled with grudging respect.

"Sorry we got off on the wrong foot." She extended her hand. "I'm Abigail."

"No problem." Lorelei shook the extended hand, secretly thrilled about touching her daughter for the first time. She played it cool, though. "Nice to meet you, Abigail. I'm Lorelei. Lorelei Sampson."

§

For the next week, Lorelei and Abigail were inseparable. They found out that they liked the same kind of music and

155

TV shows. Jason didn't seem to know that Abigail had recently got hooked on old syndicated shows. When Jason and Lorelei were alone at her house, she remarked on the similarities.

"See?" she teased. "You had no idea your own daughter was hooked on *TV Land* and *MeTV*."

He hugged her tightly.

"You're right. I didn't know she was that deep off into them. Now that I know you're her mother, I'm seeing a lot of the same traits. She likes the old shows, she likes fashion, she's feisty like you and she's fiercely protective. Almost to the point of being criminal. Like you." He laughed as she shoved him hard.

"You said that's in the past, remember?"

"I know, but it's still a trait. You know what else?" he asked, giving her a soft kiss.

"What?"

"She's beautiful, just like you."

She reached up and gave him a kiss on the lips, snuggling deeper into his arms.

"Jason, when are we going to tell her?"

"We'll know when the time is right. It's going to have to be soon because she's already asking if I've found anything out in my search. It hasn't been easy delaying her with excuses. So she won't feel too betrayed, it has to be soon."

Lorelei sighed. "Just when she's getting to like me, she's going to hate me all over again."

He squeezed her and rubbed her shoulders.

"Don't think like that. You never know."

§

The next day, Lorelei and Abby were out picking apples while Jason was at the office.

"Are you from New York or New Jersey like Dad?"

"Yes, I am originally from Brooklyn, New York. How did you know?"

"Because the way you speak around him sounds different. He sounds like he's from up there a lot to me lately. I think it's from being around you."

"I hadn't noticed."

Abby looked pensive as she picked a few more apples.

"For what it's worth, I think you're okay, Lorelei."

Lorelei held her breath and savored her words. She didn't know how much that could change once Abigail discovered the truth.

"Thanks, Abby. I think you're more than okay, too."

They talked about New York, Chicago, television, fashion and food. Abby was a few inches taller than Lorelei but still considered short. They talked about dealing with mean "tall" people.

"How did you deal with it? Was it a problem?" Abby said.

"It was…but I didn't deal with it well."

"What do you mean?"

Lorelei hesitated, wondering how much she should reveal to this teenager that was already looking up to her.

"When I was your age, I didn't handle things the right way. I was angry all of the time. I reacted in a way that was all wrong. Because I was bullied, I became a bully."

157

Abby's was in awe of her confession.

"Really? I was the same way for a while. My dad found out and I got in trouble. He started making me serve in church more and read my bible," she said, laughing.

Lorelei was on the verge of tears.

"You don't know how blessed you are for having a parent that cared enough to steer you in the right direction."

"Yeah, but I wished I'd had a mom at the time."

Her heart was wrenched by Abby's words. She held in her anguish.

"Even though she wasn't there... be glad you had a parent that cared."

A tear slipped unknowingly down Lorelei's cheek while Abby stared in stunned silence.

"Believe me - it's better to have one parent who cared, than to have two that didn't. Always remember that, Abigail," she said gravely as her voice wavered.

"I will," Abby answered softly.

§

Abby and Lorelei settled into a routine of picking apples and then going into the house for lunch. One day they were upstairs in the master bedroom when Lorelei reached into her drawer to pull out a tank top. As she pulled it out, the purple sachet fell to the floor.

*Darn, I must not have pushed it to the back.*

It didn't escape Abby's notice and she picked it up immediately. Her eyes were alight in interest as she started to open it.

"What's this?"

Lorelei hurriedly snatched the sachet out of Abby's hands. Dumbfounded, Abby stared at her in question.

"It's...nothing. It's just something from a long time ago."

Now, even more curious, Abby's eyes grew wide in innocence as she looked at Lorelei.

"Can I see it?" she asked sweetly.

Her look was bewitching. Had Lorelei used this tactic? This had to be a trick that Jason had fallen prey to often.

Panicked and with her heart beginning to race, Lorelei scrambled for more excuses. Her defenses were beginning to crumble.

"It's very private and very personal."

Abigail's face crumpled like she was hurt. That was the last thing Lorelei wanted to do, fake or not.

"I'll show you later," Lorelei said.

Abby's eyes lit up. "You promise?"

"I promise."

Then Abby's face morphed into a smirk. "You have a lot of secrets, don't you, Lorelei?"

She was taken aback by her abrupt change and straightforward words. She could be a little monster like herself, she thought. Jason was right. DNA was amazing.

Abby was shaking her head in suspicion. Regardless, she didn't want Abby to think badly of her for longer than necessary. She decided that honesty was the best tactic.

"I do. And I want to share them with you. But I need to be ready to tell you everything."

# CHAPTER TWENTY TWO

Deciding that it was time, she called Jason that night and told him what Abby had found. They decided to meet at her house after he got off work tomorrow.

The next day, Lorelei cooked Jason's favorite smothered pork chops. Abby baked an apple pie that she had learned how make when she was eight.

Afterwards, they watched TV. After the sitcom was over, Jason abruptly switched off the television.

"Aw, Dad, *Dynasty* was coming on next and me and Lorelei love that show."

"Well, if it's a rerun, you'll see it again. DVR it."

She pouted.

"Lorelei and I need to talk to you."

"About what?"

"About...things."

That got her attention. She got off the floor and went to sit on the big sofa. Jason and Lorelei were on the love seat. Abigail seemed to be getting accustomed to their intimacy.

"Alright."

Jason took a deep breath.

"Remember what you had me research a few weeks ago?" Abigail's eyes lit up in remembrance and excitement.

"Yes, about my mom..." then she looked at Lorelei as if she had given too much away, "about the matter I asked about," she backpedaled. She looked over at Lorelei in confusion. "But Dad, we can talk about that later," she said, her expression indicating that she thought it was a private matter between the two of them.

"I know what you're thinking, but this concerns Lorelei, too."

Abigail looked bewildered and was speechless for a moment.

"Why?" she asked slowly.

Deciding not to dive right into it, Jason began telling the story from the beginning.

"Remember when I told you about your grandmother and that you were originally brought home to be my little sister?"

"Yes, and then you found out that I was really your daughter."

"That's right. Well, you were conceived when I was young. A teenager."

"I know that Dad, I can add and subtract. You were fooling around with girls at my age. So you can't say too much if I start fooling around-"

"Abigail Scott, this is not the time for that. And I'd better not hear about you fooling around with *any* boys."

Lorelei suppressed a giggle at the direction the conversation was headed. She wanted to laugh. This girl was too smooth.

"I know. Sorry," Abby said under her breath.

Jason cleared his throat.

"Like I was saying, yes, I made some mistakes in high school. That doesn't excuse you to make the same ones. Are we clear?"

"Yes, Dad," she said impatiently, urging him to get to the point.

"Well, that means that I wasn't alone, obviously. I found out that the mother was someone who was in trouble at the time, and because of circumstances, gave you up for adoption. It was only by God's grace that you ended up back with me."

"I've heard the story before. You said it was a miracle that I just so happened to be back with my biological father."

"That's right."

"So where's my mother?"

"I'm getting to that. I found your birth mother a few weeks ago and I want you to know that she's had a hard time. She's had some things happen to her in high school that caused her to make a decision to give you up for adoption. And you need to remember God's grace and be forgiving. You may not understand every reason but you have to forgive."

At this point, Abby was sighing up towards the ceiling.

"I know this Dad. Are you saying all this in front of Lorelei because she's my mother or something?" Abby said, laughing.

Lorelei and Jason looked at each other in shock. Seeing their reaction, Abby's laughter abruptly faltered.

She stared at them and waited to hear more. Her face began to crumple in disbelief.

"No way!" Abby got up and ran out the room, crying.

Jason jumped up and ran after her. Meanwhile, Lorelei was left sitting on the sofa, frozen. This was all so surreal.

§

Abby was balled up in a fetal position in the first floor bedroom of the coach house.

"Talk to me, Abby."

"Dad, what are you saying?" She cried out from under her arm. "Lorelei...is...my mom?"

He handed her the birth certificate as she peeked out.

She was shaking like a leaf as she scanned the document.

"Yes, it's true. But why don't you come out and let us explain?"

She sat up abruptly, her face contorted with rage and tears.

"Explain what? How she gave me up for adoption and didn't want me? Now she's back after all of these years and trying to snag you as well? I don't get it."

He tried to remain calm. He knew how it would look to her.

"Please, Abigail. I know this is a big shock. But remember, you said you wanted me to look. And I know it sounds crazy that she and I ended up together, but please - come out and let us explain. It's a big shock to us, too."

Abigail reluctantly let herself be led out to the living room where a shaken Lorelei was still on the sofa wringing her hands and weeping silently.

"Don't even try it! How could you?" Abigail said when she spotted her.

"I'm sorry, I'm so sorry...I'm so sorry," Lorelei muttered as she rocked back and forth in anguish.

163

"It's a little too late for that now, don't you think, Lorelei?" she spat.

Jason shouted, "Sit your butt down right now, Abby. Listen to what we have to say."

Tears were steadily streaming down Abby's face as she sat down on the sofa, hugging herself tightly. Jason could see that she was terrified about the change of events.

Jason sat down next to Lorelei and patted her hand to proceed.

Abby refused to look their way.

"Abigail...please let me explain," Lorelei started.

"Make it quick."

Lorelei faltered. "I can't make it quick. It's not a quick story."

Abby stomped her foot on the ground hard.

"Whatever. I don't need this right now." She began to wail as she got up to leave.

"No. Sit..back... down... now!" Jason bellowed.

She obediently sat back down.

"Tell her, Lorelei. Tell her everything."

Lorelei sniffled as she began.

"I told you yesterday that I had secrets. Well, this was the big one. I told you I was angry all of the time when I was younger. I really don't have any excuses for what happened. I can only tell you how I felt at the time. Remember when I told you...it's better to have one parent who cared than to have two that didn't? I was talking about the relationship with my parents."

Despite her obstinacy, Lorelei had Abby's attention.

"I'm not trying to turn this into a sob story, because it's not. I was old enough to make my own decisions and they were bad decisions. My parents never showed me much affection because they were always busy, so I got it from where I thought I could. That included dealing with different boys. Even though I can't remember everything, obviously, your father was one of them. I'm not proud of it, but it's the truth. One day, I was…violated-"

"She was raped," Jason interrupted.

Abby's eyes widened in shock.

"I was…raped. I didn't know I was pregnant until it was too late and truthfully…I didn't know who…who the father was. I blamed it all on that guy…and….I didn't want to keep the baby. Since I was already too far along, my mother convinced me to have the baby and give it up for adoption. I'm not blaming it all on her because I had a choice." She said, pointing to herself.

Lorelei started weeping again and continued. "I'm just trying to tell you the truth, Abigail and how I felt at the time. I didn't want you at first. I'm sorry. But then in my seventh month, I saw a glimpse of you on the ultrasound. I was so happy… I went out and bought you this," she reached across and handed Abby the purple sachet that had been down under a pillow, "but ultimately, I didn't keep you. I thought you would be better off with parents that could love you and support you the right way. I knew I was making the biggest mistake of my life, but I was too selfish. I was a very stupid girl and I'm sorry."

Abby opened the sachet and took out the head band. She fingered it for a moment, her eyes watery with tears. Then

165

she pulled out the remaining contents. It was a yellowed ultrasound scan.

"Is this me?"

Lorelei smiled through her tears while Jason hugged her tight.

"Yes."

Abby's face crumpled again while holding the picture. Jason went to Abby and held his daughter.

"Why didn't you want me? I needed a mommy... so bad." She hiccupped.

That only devastated Lorelei more. "I'm sorry, I'm here now?" she cried.

Abigail wrenched herself free from her Dad's arms.

"It's too late now. I'm almost an adult." She valiantly wiped her face and got up to leave. "Thanks for telling me that pathetic story. I only wanted to know who you were. I don't need a mother. I don't need you and I don't want to hear anymore."

Abigail ran out the house while Lorelei held her face in her hands, weeping loudly.

Jason turned back to Lorelei.

"Sorry, Lorie, I need to go after her."

She shooed him away without looking up.

"Yes, she needs you. Go."

§

At home, he went up to Abby's bedroom and knocked on the door.

"Please, Dad. I can't deal with this right now."

166

"I know. Just let me talk to you for a minute."

When she didn't answer, he opened the door softly. She was lying on top of the bed in the same fetal position at the coach house.

"I just want to explain some things to you." He came and sat on the edge of the bed.

She sat up. "Dad, how did she find her way here? I don't understand. We saw her floating in the river."

"I know. So she didn't come looking for us. Remember how I told you that I believe in divine appointments?"

She nodded.

"Well, this is definitely one. Think about it. If we had been a few minutes too late when we were strolling down the boardwalk that night, that woman who is your mother would've been dead. And when I did the search that you asked me to do, it would've traced back to a deceased drowning victim. The fact that we were there to save her - this is not a coincidence."

Abby looked pensive while he spoke. He knew she was grasping the gravity of his words and he knew she believed in God.

"What are the chances of Lorelei and I starting a romance, and then to find out that we already have a child together? That we're both your biological parents? Do you know how crazy that sounds?"

"Yeah. It does." She was quiet for a moment. "Dad, I need time to process all of this. This is too much."

"I know it is. It took both of us a while to process it."

He gave her a kiss on the temple and got up to leave. Before he closed the door, she softly called out.

TRACI MORRIS

"Daddy, do you really care for her? I mean - is she the one?"

"Sweetheart, I really believe she's the one. And she didn't come here with any ulterior motives. She had no idea that this would happen. Her intentions are true and she's also accepted a relationship with Christ. This was all before I got the documents back from Mark and told her the truth. So please, consider that. Consider this a miracle that she's here."

She was quiet, no doubt taking it all in.

"By the way, Lorie named you Abigail."

She stared into her father's eyes in surprise and put her head down into her hands.

"I can't make any promises, Dad, but okay, I'll think about everything you said."

"That's fine, baby girl. That's all I want you to do."

## CHAPTER TWENTY THREE

Abby left early the next morning. When Jason got up to leave for work, he received a text before calling out to let her know he was leaving for work.

*Dad,*
*Sorry. This is all too much right now and I need time away to think. I took a cab and Candice is picking me up from the train station in Savannah. I'm going to stay with her and her family for a while. I hope you don't mind. I need space.*
*Abby*

He couldn't really say he was surprised.

*That's fine, Abby. Pray on it. Keep me posted.*

*I will.*

§

Lorelei found out from Jason that Abby took off for Savannah. Although not surprised, she had to admit she was hurt. She tried to put herself in the young girl's shoes. She would feel the same way. She actually had to commend Abigail for handling it more maturely than she thought she herself would.

Jason came over after work.

As they sat on the sofa, he hugged her and gave her a kiss on the forehead. He knew she needed some affection.

"How are you today?"

She sighed. "I'm okay, I guess. I missed picking apples with Abby this morning."

"I know. She'll come around eventually."

"I think she handled it better than I would. That's for sure."

"I told her that you named her and I think it helped."

Leaning away, she looked up at him in surprise and hope. "Really?"

"Yeah. I also explained that since we found you the way that we did, you have no ulterior motive. And how it couldn't have been a coincidence that the woman we rescued was her mother. I told her how we could've been too late."

Lorelei shivered at his words. They could've been too late and she never would've met her true love and her daughter. God was awesome.

"I think she's pretty level headed and will consider all of these factors," he said.

She leaned back into him.

"I hope so. In the last week, I've grown very attached to her."

"Let's just give her time."

§

Weeks passed with no return from Abby. She texted Jason a few times to let him know she was fine, but that was it.

Jason and Lorelei fell back into their normal routine. That included making out on the sofa.

One evening, he had to pull away, his breath ragged.

"We have some decisions to make. This is becoming a task."

"What is?"

"Abstaining. I want you so much."

She laughed. "Well, let's go upstairs."

"I want to but I'm trying to do the right thing."

"Well, what is the right thing?"

"You know what the right thing is."

She truly looked baffled.

"The right thing would be for you to marry me."

She looked around and laughed as if he had just made a joke.

"Are you serious?"

Jason wasn't laughing. "I'm very serious."

Her insecurity kicked in.

"But, why? After all I've done, why would you want to marry *me*?" She asked.

"Oh...maybe because - I love you?" he said, giving her a forehead kiss.

Her heart was ready to burst.

"Jason..."

"Before you say anything, let me finish," he asked. She nodded and he continued. "I know we've only been together a few months and we've gotten the biggest shock of our lives. But I believe this is where we were destined to be. I believe that through many false starts, edits, and detours on

171

our journey, we were meant to be. We found our way back. Why wait?"

Her eyes filled with tears. He was really serious.

"Lorelei, do you love me?"

She hesitated. She had never confessed love to anyone that was real. If she bared herself to him, her heart would be completely in his hands to crush at will.

He mistook her hesitation for uncertainty.

"Maybe I was mistaken…"

"No, no, you aren't. It's just that I've never felt so vulnerable. I've put up so many fronts for so long just to protect myself from pain. Hear me out."

She cleared her throat and turned completely towards him.

"Jason Derrick Scott. I love you so very much." His expression went from surprise to relief to happiness. "I've loved you for a while now and I've never really loved anyone else. Please know that."

He contemplated her genuine expression. His heart was so full.

"Alright. Why do you love me?" he asked, giving her a butterfly kiss on her temple.

"Because you've taught me not to take myself so seriously, you make me laugh, you're devastatingly sexy-"

"Yeah, keep going," he murmured, kissing towards her mouth.

She giggled and then sobered.

"You've accepted me for who I am – gigantic, massive flaws and all, you've helped me in so many ways and showed me that I could have a higher quality life with God…and…" she trailed off, her voice catching.

"And?" he prompted.

"And, you've done one fantastic job of raising our daughter." She tried to keep from breaking down but was unsuccessful. She had been doing too much of that, lately. A tear involuntarily came to his eyes.

"I couldn't ask for a better parent to have raised her." She grabbed his hand. "Thank you so much."

He took her into his arms and allowed her to weep.

"Thank you for bravely giving birth to our baby girl."

"I don't deserve that, Jason. I would've had an ab…I wouldn't have kept her if I had known in time."

"I know that. But you were too late. And you gave birth to her anyway. I can't be absolved either. I was irresponsible. Stop viewing me like the angel in all of this."

"Okay. You're right."

He threw his hands up.

"Look. Are we going to beat ourselves up for the rest of our lives or are we going to forgive our mistakes like God has forgiven them?"

"Forgive ourselves."

"So, let's get married and have a family. We already got started years ago. Let's finish this thing."

She laughed and they hugged each other.

§

Abby came back a week after they made the decision to get married. She didn't look at Abby as Jason dragged her into the coach house.

"We have something to tell you."

Abby slapped her forehead and plopped down on the sofa. "Oh no, not another bombshell. Do I need a drink?"

"Hey!" Jason bellowed.

Already geared up for Abby's attitude and well stocked up on her Word, Lorelei laughed heartily.

Abby looked at her in scorn. "What's your problem?" Abby asked.

Lorelei walked over to Abby and sweetly sat down.

"I know you've had a big shock finding out about everything. I'm very sorry you had to go through that." Her voice rose. "But the time for you being rude to me and talking to me any old kind of way – IS OVER!" she roared.

Both Abby and Jason looked at Lorelei in surprise. Jason started chuckling. Abby looked at her father in confusion.

"Dad? Who does she think she is talking to me like that?"

"Well, according to your birth certificate, she's your mother."

"But I haven't accepted her as my mom, yet."

"I tell you what. You may not have accepted her as your mom, but you'll have to accept her as your stepmom."

"What?"

Jason sat down next to Lorelei and took her hand in his. They both smiled broadly.

"We're getting married," they said in unison.

Throwing her hands up, Abby sighed and leaned back onto the sofa.

§

After spending more time in the Word, Lorelei had a peace about everything that had happened and would happen. Instead of worrying sick what Abby thought or if she would come around, she decided to give it over to the Lord. I Peter 5:7 said, *casting all your anxiety on Him, because He cares for you.* No matter what happened, she would be at peace.

After their announcement, Abby went back to the other house and they didn't see her for the rest of the evening.

§

The next day, Lorelei was out picking apples and humming a tune of praise. She felt content and happy. After all, she would be marrying her true love. She was in awe of God's mercy and grace. What was more, she had called her tech people and was told the video hadn't resurfaced in months. They believed it was scrapped for good. For the first time in her life, she felt truly blessed.

"Hi," a voice softly greeted.

She turned around in surprise at Abby and smiled pleasantly at her daughter.

"Hi, Abigail. How are you this morning?"

Abby began picking up apples instead of answering her. That was fine with Lorelei. She continued humming and picking apples. She could play this game since she had done the same thing when she was younger. Genetics were a trip. After a few moments of silence, Abby cleared her throat.

"I just wanted to say, congratulations."

Lorelei was pleasantly surprised. "Thank you, Abigail."

"Yeah...and...I give you my blessing."

"Thank you very much."

"I liked you before I found out...before I found out...you know. I already thought you were cool and good for my dad, so...I don't see any reason to interfere with him being happy. I love my dad..." her face crumpled, "and I just want him to be happy..." She burst into tears.

At first, Lorelei wasn't sure what to do but decided to go on instinct. She dropped her basket and took the girl in her arms. It didn't matter that she was slightly taller than Lorelei. This was her baby.

She expected for Abby to resist her but she fell heavily into Lorelei's arms. They stood like that for several moments, Lorelei stroking her hair and consoling her. Lorelei began to cry at how good it felt to finally hold her baby.

"Come on, let's go sit."

Lorelei led Abby over to the steps of the front porch and they sat down. Abby wiped her eyes.

Bravely, Lorelei asked, "What's on your mind, Abby?"

Abby hesitated, looking down at her feet.

"I've always wondered about my real mom and that's why I told Dad that I was ready to look for her. For years after Gina left, even though I didn't really connect with her, it made me think that something was wrong with me. I couldn't understand why I didn't have a mother who loved me like most of my friends did. So when I found out about you, I was immediately suspicious. It didn't occur to me at

LORELEI: OFF: THE CHAIN

first that by the way we discovered you, there was no way you could've planned it. I'm sorry."

"I understand. I want to commend you on the way you took the news. I would've probably handled it much worse at your age. You're way more mature than I ever was."

"Really? Tell me about your childhood."

Lorelei sighed and told her about everything including the bullying, the lack of affection from her parents, the promiscuity with boys, the failed engagements and anything else she wanted to know. She even acquired the guts to mention the sex tape to her. She had nothing left to lose. She was trying to gain. They talked for hours and Lorelei confessed it all.

"I don't have any excuses, but that was what I became."

"But I can understand why. Your parents were horrible to you."

"Yeah, they were definitely lacking, but I still could've made better decisions."

Abby was quiet. "How do you feel about me?"

Lorelei's heart broke at the question.

"Oh, sweetheart. I've loved you since the day I saw your ultrasound. I just buried it because it was so painful. It was always there, that's why I was so evil. I was trying to replace my broken heart with things and it never worked. I know that you're fifteen and don't need a mother, but I would love to be here for you. I don't have a good relationship with my mother and I would love to break that generational curse and at least be friends."

Abby launched herself into Lorelei's arms. They held on tight as they both wept.

"I lied. I do." Abby murmured through tears.

"Do what?"

"I need a mother, Mom."

Lorelei's heart was about to burst with pure joy. Abigail was accepting her! And she had called her something she was never able to call her mother. *Mom.* Abby had called her *Mom*! After fifteen years, she had her daughter back.

God was so awesome!

"Oh, sweetheart. I'll never let you go again," Lorelei sobbed.

They didn't let each other go for a long time and rocked until the sun began to set.

§

That evening, Jason came over the coach house to see his two girls sitting close, eating popcorn together on the sofa and watching *Dallas* reruns. His heart was so full.

*Praise The Lord. We can finally be a real family.*

# RELEASED

## PART VII

### CHAPTER TWENTY FOUR

Not wanting anything too elaborate, Jason and Lorelei were wed at the county courthouse later that August. Since she had a new lease on life, she wanted to do everything the opposite of how she might've done in her old, past, empty life.

She and Abby dressed up in romantic, short ivory dresses with simple rose and lily bouquets, her bouquet slightly more elaborate. She wore her hair down like Abby's with minimal makeup, just how Jason liked it. Jason was dressed in a tan suit and looked very dashing, his dimples ever present. All three of them marched up the courtroom steps and into the hall, holding hands. The county judge who was the officiator, smiled.

"You look like a readymade family."

The three of them laughed.

Abby said, "We are. These are my parents that didn't know they had me together and they're getting married, fifteen years later. Talk about readymade!"

Chuckling, the judge looked confused and just shook his head.

"Don't even try to figure it out," Jason quipped.

"I won't."

He proceeded with the one minute and fifteen second ceremony and the two were married. It was over that quick.

"I now pronounce you man and wife."

Lorelei and Jason leaned in and gave each other a long sensual kiss.

"Eww, Mom and Dad - I'm still in the room."

"Shut up. How do you think you got here," Lorelei snapped playfully.

Abby giggled.

§

Lorelei was a bit anxious about their first night as a married couple because of her past.

She remembered a conversation they'd had about sex...

"I think it was really a means to an end for me. I liked the closeness that would sometimes occur afterwards more so than the act. After the incident in high school, I could totally do without it and I did. Once I was engaged, I tried again but didn't care for it. Too many bad memories. I think that's why he strayed elsewhere. I still tried to hold out hope because I was fond of him. I took whatever type of attention I could get. I was foolish."

"What happened with Andrew?"

"We didn't have that type of relationship at all. He was more like a little brother to me and still had a girlfriend he cared for. I didn't really care one way or another. That's why I got with that guy..."

"The guy from the tape debacle." he added.

"Yes. What's ironic is that incident makes me look like some type of sex fiend which is the furthest from the truth.

That was my first time in years." She sat up to look at him. "For goodness sake, my nickname around town was *The Ice Princess*. It was already rumored that I was frigid," she said, shaking her head. "So, yeah, I never really enjoyed it very much."

He thought about what she said and chuckled.

"Never enjoyed it, huh? Obviously I didn't make a good first impression on you back in high school since you don't remember much," he chortled. "Since I have more experience now, hopefully it will be better to you," he teased.

She swatted him and they laughed. "Stop it Jason, you were probably just fine back then. I just didn't like sex that much, period. I think I remember you smelled good. Those are the type of things I would remember about a guy. I was going to look you up but…things happened."

He hugged her tight and she luxuriated in his tender loving care. He felt so good to her.

"I plan on hugging and squeezing on you for the rest of my life. I'll make up for what you didn't have."

Tipping her chin up, he kissed her sensually, giving her shivers, something that had never happened with anyone.

"And I'm going to show you how good it *all* can be."

"I'm sure you will." She said, reaching up to kiss him softly.

§

They had decided that Lorelei would move into the bigger house now that they were married. She wasn't too happy

181

with that decision because she had grown to love her quaint little space.

"We can split our time between the two. How's that?" Jason offered.

"You mean when we have arguments, I can run over here?" She asked, laughing.

"No, we don't go to sleep with any arguments over our head. Remember, Ephesians 4:26 says, *Do not let the sun go down while you are still angry.*"

She had just learned that in Bible study last night.

"I had forgotten that verse that quick."

He took her in his arms and gave her a kiss before heading downstairs.

"That happens. I'll be right back."

That evening, Abby opted to stay alone in the other house while Lorelei and Jason spent their wedding night in the coach house. Next week, Abby would be returning to school. They didn't want to cut into any family time, so they decided to honeymoon in Bermuda after she left.

§

She waited for Jason to come back upstairs after turning off the lights. Now in his bathrobe, he cautiously sat on the edge of the bed. Lorelei was lying on the bed with the covers pulled up to her neck.

"What's wrong, baby?" he asked softly.

"I guess I'm still nervous." She shook her head in frustration. "I keep being reminded of my past."

He looked at her and smiled. "Do you love me?"

"Yes."

"Then that's all that we need. We have God's blessing and we're brand new creatures. Get that other garbage out of your head. That's just the enemy telling you you're not worthy of true love and he is a liar. I'm your husband and I love you very, very much. Don't ever forget that. I'm yours, completely."

She reached up to put her arms around his neck, kissing his cheek.

"You are so wonderful to me. I'm so thankful to have found someone like you, Jason Derrick Scott. Thank you."

"Same to you, Mrs. Lorelei Scott."

She giggled at her new name. She wasn't planning on going by a hyphenated name or anything like that - just his last name. Sampson, a name she haughtily threw around for the sake of status, was now a name she was glad to lose. She wanted him and everyone else to know that she was completely and utterly his. So honored was she to be his wife. He was the only man who had ever truly loved her.

His head lowered as their lips met. He pulled the covers slowly down and switched off the light. He could still see her clearly in the darkness. The moon shone brightly on them.

"The marriage bed is undefiled, so let's just enjoy ourselves, mmmm?" he said huskily. "Just pretend we're downstairs on the sofa, but this time, we don't have to stop."

She giggled at his suggestion and relaxed.

He started with her face, giving her sensual butterfly pecks. He slowly removed the covers from up around her.

They kissed languidly and slowly. He made sure to take his time so that she would be at ease. They had all night.

He made his way down to her neck. She could feel his hunger increasing as he nipped her throat down to her collarbone. Once he reached her chest, he removed her lingerie and languidly kissed and squeezed her with both of his strong hands. She was enraptured by what he was doing to her. She writhed on the bed and groaned in pleasure as she watched the way his tongue played with her. She had never seen or felt anything so sensual.

After slowly removing the rest of the lingerie, he kissed her in places she had never been kissed before. She was bucking and thrashing as he held her still.

"No one has ever kissed you like this before?" He murmured up at her.

"No, never," she moaned.

"Idiots," he mumbled as he continued his feast on every part of her. She was mad with ecstasy as she gazed down at him. She had been wrong. She had never seen or felt anything as sensual as *this*.

Erupting almost immediately into unspeakable bliss, it was forever before her body stopped its trembling, and she descended back to planet earth.

Eventually, he moved back up her body and looked deeply into her eyes which shone in wonder.

"Are you enjoying yourself, my love?"

Her brain began to function again.

"Oh, yes."

"Just what I want to hear. Hold on, baby."

She put her arms around his neck in anticipation of what was to come next. He looked deeply into her eyes as they joined in one motion. They gasped in pleasure and surprise and marveled their union.

*What a man.*

She gasped as he filled her completely, rolling them gently. He looked into her eyes with intense emotion.

"Lorie, you were specifically designed for me and no one else. You didn't know it but you were waiting for me, again. That's why you've never been satisfied."

She trembled at gravity of his words as she held onto his muscular shoulders to brace herself for what was to come. She was completely overwhelmed. All of her five senses and soul were consumed with nothing but Jason. Jason squeezed her body up to his and gave her all that he had. He surrounded her and enveloped her completely. She felt wanton as Jason drove her to pleasures she never thought possible.

So, this was making love? Immediately, she received revelation that it was only meant for people who loved each other. She had never felt anything close to this. It was one of the greatest highs of her life. She gasped as he rocked her repeatedly on his way to rapidly. They were soaring up to the moon and she could see the stars. She mewled and cried out repeatedly as they went higher and higher.

"That's right, let me know you love it."

Just from his words, Lorelei felt herself building to unspeakable pleasure. Jason accelerated as he anticipated their impending rapture. Apparently loving how petite and easy she was to maneuver, he changed their poses again and again. She was becoming exhausted as he kept them from reaching their impending rapture.

"Jason," she pleaded.

"I just want it to be good to you."

"It is. It is," she moaned.

She whimpered as his movements became even more erratic. Lorelei splintered like a volcano as he took her there. She had never felt such intense pleasure. It took a hold and didn't release her for an eternity. Jason continued to rock them until they cried out together as he crashed. He groaned in satisfaction as he stilled. He continued burrowing in while he nipped the side of her throat and down to her chest. Once he laid them back down, she hazily looked at him with so much love in her eyes.

"You are amazing," he said and kissed her softly on the forehead.

"So are you."

She slowly drifted away.

As she regained awareness, she was in his arms. He was gazing at her with intense emotion.

She reached up to kiss him and once again their passion reignited. That night, they continued to give into their every pleasure as they made love until the dawn. With a blessed union that was sanctified by God, Lorelei had never had more peace in her life.

## CHAPTER TWENTY FIVE

The following week, Abby left for another semester. Mother and daughter held on tight before Abby left to get on the train.

"Stop crying, Mom. I'll be back for Thanksgiving."

"I know you will. But I'll still miss you. I just got you."

She hugged her mother even tighter.

"I know. I'll miss you, too. Text me. Okay?"

"I will."

Lorelei wiped her tears as she watched Jason and Abby hug after he carried her bags onto the train.

They stood together and waved while the train slowly took off.

"Bye, Mom and Dad." Abby cheesed hard, apparently liking the way that sounded.

Jason and Lorelei cheesed even harder. They *loved* the way it sounded.

§

Little did Abby know that she was in for a surprise almost as soon as she left for school. The week after they returned from their short honeymoon in Bermuda, Lorelei scrambled to make arrangements for the following weekend. She and Jason had contacted every one of Abby's friends, entrusting Candice with the task of making up a story to bring her home the following Saturday.

When Abby came through the door of the Coach House with Candice, she was greeted with a loud roar.

"Surprise!"

Abby looked around to see about fifteen of her friends in the living room with birthday hats on. She looked over and saw the huge birthday banner on the wall.

Her parents came over and kissed her while Abby started to cry tears of happiness.

"Happy Sweet Sixteen, baby," they said together.

"You didn't think we forgot, did you?" Jason asked as she hugged them.

"Mom, Dad, how did you do all this?"

"Well, this was your mom's idea and she did all of the planning and decorations. I couldn't stop her once she got the idea in her head. I just contacted everyone whose numbers I had and told them to call everyone else."

She looked around at her friends who were milling around, drinking punch and eating appetizers.

"Mom, this is so nice. I thought I was just going to have a quiet birthday at school and hang out with friends or something."

Jason scoffed. "Have I *ever* missed your birthday?"

Abby laughed. "No, Dad. I just thought you'd be "preoccupied," she finger-quoted, "with Mom."

They laughed.

Lorelei said, "Well, I've missed the last fourteen birthdays, and I didn't want to miss another."

"Baby, you mean fifteen, right?" Jason asked Lorelei.

"No. Remember, I was actually there for the first." Abby's eyes watered along with Lorelei.

"I guess that's true, Touché" Jason said. "You've been doing some critical thinking."

All three of them laughed.

Abby went around and greeted her friends, hugging and thanking them for coming. She led Candice back to Lorelei.

"Mom, I'm not sure if you've met my best friend, Candice. Candice, this is my mom."

"Hi, Candice. Pleased to meet you in the flesh."

Abby looked puzzled.

"We talked over the phone to plan how to get you here."Lorelei laughed.

"That's right, Candy. You tricked me!" Abby exclaimed, nudging her best friend. Meanwhile, Candice looked at Lorelei in wonder."

"Wow, Abby, you look a lot like your mom. I'm sorry for staring, Mrs. Scott. It's just that Abby told me the awesome stuff that's been happening with you guys and it's so amazing to hear. I'm so happy for you, Abby and Dr. Scott."

Abby looked down, shuffling her feet. "Yeah, she's the one who finally convinced me that life was too short and to go back home. She basically kicked me out of her house."

"Thank you, Candice." Lorelei gave her a warm hug.

That day, Abby led Lorelei around and proudly introduced her to everyone as her mom, even though she had met them before Abby got there. She didn't mind. It meant her daughter was proud of her. If that's what it meant, she would gladly meet each one of them again and again.

Amazed and thankful, Jason stood over in the corner, taking it all in. He was crazy about his two girls and ecstatic that they were already crazy about each other.

§

They honeymooned only a few days in Bermuda because of Abby's party and Jason actually needed to get back to work. He had a few patients approaching delivery that he wanted to make sure he was around for, just in case.

Lorelei was just fine being back home. She had traveled to plenty of islands in the past and felt that as long as she was with Jason, it didn't matter where they were.

"I think I want to go back to school soon," Lorelei announced.

"Great. For what? Nursing?"

"I'm thinking about trying to get a certification as a midwife."

He looked at her in surprise. "Really? Wow. That's a wonderful idea, baby. You were a great help that day. I know you can do it."

She basked in the compliment from such a competent physician as her husband.

"Thank you, Jason. I don't know if I told you, but I think you're an amazing doctor."

He blasted her with his mega white dimpled smile that slayed her every time. "Thank you, love."

He helped her look up schools in Savannah that she could attend the following year.

She had narrowed it down to two or three.

"What are we going to do about the apples?"

"Well, I was already in the process of looking for someone to help out Duke. Right now I think you should focus on learning all you can about it to make sure it's what you really want to do."

She'd already had a stack of books she'd been scouring through regarding the subject of midwifery.

"That's a good idea."

In about a week, Duke had a young assistant in his twenties, Danny, to help out with the harvesting.

§

Jason hadn't told anyone at the practice about the miraculous discovery that Lorelei was really Abby's mom. He felt that it was something that Lorelei would have to divulge if she wanted to. He was fine with letting everyone believe that Abby just had a new stepmom.

They came to the practice together one day.

"I knew she was the one. Congratulations. Too bad I couldn't see you two lovebirds tie the knot," Dr. Lillian teased.

"Sorry about that, Lil. No one did. It was just the three of us." Jason said apologetically.

"Aww, I think that's very sweet."

"We have pictures, though," Lorelei offered.

"Ooh, let me see."

Everyone in the practice gathered around as Lorelei and Jason showed off their scrapbook of professional pictures taken in the orchard after the wedding.

The three of them looked blissfully happy.

"Wow, Abby and Lorelei look uncannily alike," Rose remarked.

Jason and Lorelei shared a secret smile.

"And they act alike, too." Jason added with a smirk.

§

Lorelei was joining Jason at the practice more often to help out and learn from Rose. Rose was ecstatic to hear about Lorelei's new ambition because she was planning to eventually leave the practice to relocate with her fiancé.'

In Lorelei's research, she discovered there were about three or four different paths to becoming a midwife. Since she already had a degree, becoming a Certified Midwife or a CM was the sensible path for her. Rose enthusiastically offered to be her supervisor for an apprenticeship that was required along with graduate school.

The following week, Lorelei was training with Rose and left the examination room for a bathroom break. There was a gorgeous, leggy brunette leaning across the desk, baring full cleavage to Amy, the new receptionist.

"Where is he? I'm just dropping by to say, Hi," the woman purred.

Eyes huge and feeling awkward, Amy answered politely, "He's with a patient but he should be out in a moment. Would you like to wait?"

At that moment, the woman's eyes descended on Lorelei who was standing in the doorway, frozen. She glared back at Lorelei in challenge.

"Sure, I'll wait."

She sashayed over to a seat, her dress tightly showing off all her assets.

A chill ran through Lorelei as old feelings of resentment descended on her.

She knew this chick had to be waiting for Jason. Dr. Mansfield wasn't here today.

She was immobilized with a fear that was turning into rage. She wanted to cut this trick that was obviously after her husband. Just as she was about to approach her, Jason came out to the waiting area. Lorelei stood stock still as she observed her husband who hadn't noticed her watching in the doorway.

The bimbo stood up and wiggled towards Jason.

"Hi, Jay! I was in the area and wanted to stop by and see how you were. You're looking mighty handsome, mmmm better than ever," she purred.

He gave her a tight smile. "What are you doing here, Gina?"

*Gina? His ex, Gina? She looked like that?*

Feelings of low self-esteem and immense devastation swept through Lorelei. Involuntarily, she was reminded of her experiences in school and her failed engagements. Her blood was running hot and cold.

"I told you I just wanted to see you. I've been thinking about us-"

"Look, Gina. I don't want to hear it. You need to be on your way."

She sauntered in close to him.

"What's wrong, baby? Don't you remember how good we used to be together?"

"We were never good together-"

Lorelei's back snapped into action. She marched towards Gina and grabbed her by the hair.

"Bitch, didn't you hear what he said? He's not interested!"

"Lorie!" Alarmed, Jason grabbed his wife and pried her hands away from a screeching Gina. "Lorie, calm down. I was handling this, what are you doing?"

Lorelei still hadn't quite let go.

He whispered in her ear as he managed to pull her away from Gina. "I can't believe what've you're doing. Calm down, baby." Lorelei was still kicking and resisting, trying to get back at Gina. He had to bodily pick her up and carry her to the other side of the room.

He put her down behind him to keep her away and turned back to Gina.

"Gina, that's my wife, Lorelei. As you can see, you can't just come in here throwing yourself at me. I'm married and not interested. Not now, not ever. She got a little carried away, but so did you. Don't ever come back here anymore. "

Gina stood up, fixing her hair and glaring at him and Lorelei.

"My God, Jason. What did you get yourself into with that psychotic munchkin? She's like the Tasmanian devil or something. Don't worry, I won't be back." She haughtily flung her long hair, turned on her heel and left the office.

"Good. Now beat it," he called after her.

As Lorelei realized how far she had slipped into her old self, she ran into an open exam room and sank to the floor, crying. She knew Amy thought she was nuts, too. She had embarrassed her husband at his place of business.

Jason came in after her and kneeled down on his haunches.

"Baby, are you okay? I had it under control. Why did you interfere?"

She hugged herself, tightly.

"I don't know, I don't know."

"Were you having flashbacks?"

"Jason... I don't want to talk about it right now... I messed up okay? I don't want to talk about it, please." Fresh tears streamed down her face as she rocked back and forth. This was a side she had thought was dead and buried, and although he knew about her past, she hadn't planned on him seeing her in action. She was mortified.

*So much for being a good Christian.*

He stood back up. "Okay, baby. Why don't you take the car and go home. I have a few more appointments, but I'll talk to you later." He leaned over and gave her a kiss on the head and left the room. Once she got herself together enough to leave the room, she saw Amy as she attempted to sneak out.

Amy, ever sweet and kind, called to her.

"Don't feel bad, Lorelei. I would've probably done the same thing. She was so out of order. I can't believe she had her boobs all in my face."

Lorelei smiled but was still embarrassed.

Amy leaned up and whispered, "Don't worry, nobody saw anything and I'll keep this on the hush from everyone else. I think you're totally cool."

She smiled gratefully at Amy.

"I appreciate that, Amy. Honestly, I lost it and I was wrong, but thanks anyway.

# CHAPTER TWENTY SIX

Instead of their house, she went to the coach house, finding comfortable refuge in her old bedroom. She thought about what had happened and felt like a disgrace. She figured Jason finally realized he married a raving lunatic.

*My true colors.*

She wept for hours and when he came to the house looking for her, he found that she had locked the bedroom door. He knocked but she wouldn't answer. She just couldn't face him right now.

At ten o' clock, Jason knocked on the door once more. She had fallen asleep and as soon as she heard it, she was reminded of her earlier behavior.

"Lorelei, let me in." This had to be serious if he was addressing her so formally. He probably wanted a divorce.

"Let me in or I'm unlocking the door."

Reluctantly, she got up, unlocked the door and quickly ran back to the bed to hide her face in the covers.

She felt him sit on the bed.

"Let's talk."

"I don't want to and I'm sleepy," she murmured from under her arm.

"Nope. That's not how it goes. Remember, we don't let the sun set on any disagreements. I knew when that day came, you would run over here. I told you that's not what this place is for. Do it again and I'm changing the locks on you."

He sounded so angry. This was a first. They were having their first fight.

She sat up, insecurities flaring. "How often does *she* come there?"

"She was there a few years ago and I blew her off back then, too."

She folded her arms defiantly. She was remembering the taunts and references to her stature before Gina stormed out. It only made her feel more insecure and lacking in comparison to his tall, shapely ex-wife.

"So that's the type of women you usually like, huh?" she accused.

He knew she was fragile and needed reassurance.

"Yes, she was beautiful, but we never had the connection that you and I have. She never made me feel like you do, not even close. And don't forget that I went after you years before I ever met her. So obviously, you are my type," he said, grinning at his beautifully made point.

She had to admit it was smooth, even if it was bull.

"Look, Lorie, I told you you're going to have to trust me. How long were you standing there when I came out to talk to her?"

"The whole time."

He smirked. "Did you hear me say anything wrong?"

"No," she admitted, shamefaced. "I could hear you didn't want to be bothered with her."

"Alright. So that means I had no intentions on dealing with her and you should have just trusted me and let me handle her."

She put her head in her hands.

"I know. Oh, Jason, I know I messed up… and I'm so ashamed…but I don't know what happened. I just lost it, okay? I thought I could control it but…"

"You had flashbacks."

She nodded. "I did trust you. I mean I do trust you. It's really her that I had a problem with. She reminded me of…of the type of chicks I've had to deal with for years."

He shook his head."Well, you're going to have to get over that. There are plenty of women in all shapes and sizes who like to chase doctors. I'm constantly fighting off forward women at the hospital. What are you going to do? Beat them all up?"

She chuckled bitterly.

"No. I can't do that. I'll do better, I promise. But I feel like I've let you and God down."

"Just repent and sincerely ask for forgiveness. Ask Him for help in this matter. A Believer is not a perfect person. There was only one perfect person and that's Jesus himself. That's what a lot of people fail to realize. They think we're supposed to be perfect in all that we do. And they're sitting around just waiting for us to mess up so they can justify why our way is a waste of time. But it's because we're imperfect that we need Him."

She smiled through her tears. She loved this man so much for how he was also able to make her look at the worst things in a positive light.

"That makes sense, thank you."

"You can find that out and get strength for challenges like that by reading more of your Word. I'm sorry we haven't had Bible study lately, because we need to constantly refresh our spirits so that we handle situations like today. Somewhere in 2 Timothy, first chapter, it speaks on power and love and discipline. You can meditate on that."

"Alright, I will. This whole thing made me feel terrible."

"Good. That means that despite what happened today, you're a work in progress. Would the old Lorelei have felt this bad?"

She snorted loudly, "Not even a little bit."

He laughed. "See?"

He leaned forward and kissed her, slipping her shirt down her shoulder, his eyes smoldering suggestively.

"By the way, I forgive you," he said with a soft kiss. "You know what just happened? We just had our first fight...so you know what that means?"

"What?" she asked innocently, although she knew full well what he was getting at.

"That means we have to thoroughly make up."

He eased her back into the mattress and erased all thoughts of anything or anyone else from her mind. That night, with everything that was within him, he showed her that he was completely hers.

*Thank you, God for bringing me this man.*

§

Later in October, Lorelei finally got a call from her mother. Lorelei knew she was wondering why Lorelei had been keeping quiet and hadn't been calling to ask Ed to raise her limit up again.

She barked into the phone as soon as Lorelei answered.

"Why haven't you called? What have you gotten yourself into now, tramp."

Jason took the phone out of his wife's hand. He had heard every word.

"Excuse me, Mallory, is it?"

"Who in the hell is this?"

"This is Dr. Jason Scott. I'm Lorelei's husband."

"What the f---?"

He held the phone away from his ear in amusement. Lorelei had her hand over her mouth in astonishment and amusement.

"Mrs. Sampson - please. Language!" he laughed.

For a moment, there was silence before she finally spoke.

"Oh, sorry. Seriously though, is this some kind of joke? Who are you?"

"I apologize for the shock, but I just married your daughter last month. Sorry that I didn't get to formally meet you, first."

Lorelei knew Mallory was utterly speechless.

"I just wanted to let you know that your daughter is not a tramp any longer," Lorie swatted Jason's arm, "she is my wife. Please refrain from such terms. It is a dishonor to her and to me. I hope to meet you soon. Goodbye."

Jason gave the phone back to Lorelei as he fell over onto the bed, holding his stomach and laughing silently.

She giggled and tried to be serious when she retrieved the phone. She knew Mallory was about to be apoplectic.

"Mallory-"

"Lorelei! What in the hell is going on? What have you done? Who was that? Are you out of your mind?"

She calmly answered.

"No, Mallory. That was really my husband. His name is Jason Scott and we love each other very much."

"No way. Someone really loves you? *You?* He must not know all about you. Why did you marry him? Is he wealthy? Did you say he was a doctor? What kind?"

"He's an obstetrician. And believe me, he knows all about me."

"Ok, ok, whatever. Hmmm, I guess obstetricians do alright. Why didn't you set your sights on a surgeon or an anesthesiologist? They make the big bucks-"

"Mallory! I didn't marry Jason for money. We love each other. I know that's hard for you to believe, but it's true. I'm a changed woman. I've also accepted Christ into my life..."

At this, Mallory dropped the phone and erupted into high pitched laughter. This went on for about two minutes. Jason and Lorelei looked at each other and shook their heads.

Jason reached out to hug his wife.

"I'm so sorry, baby. I'm sorry for what you had to go through."

A tear slipped down her face. She was so grateful that she had him and Abby. Now he knew what she'd had to deal with all these years.

After another minute of Mallory's cackles, they hung up.

# FREEDOM

## PART VIII

### CHAPTER TWENTY SEVEN

Lorelei didn't hear from her mother again, but Ed called.
He was hesitant, as if he wasn't sure how to talk to her. Truthfully, they'd never really had a one on one conversation. Mallory was always an ever present albatross.

"Hi, Lorie." Her father still occasionally called her that. He laughed nervously. "Mal tells me you got married to some doctor. Is that true?"

"Yes, Ed. His name is Jason Scott and we love each other very much. We're very happy and being down here has changed my life."

He was silent for a moment.

"Well, I'm happy to hear that. Uh…congratulations."

Her heart fluttered to hear it coming from her father. He'd never really been mean to her, just indifferent.

"I've decided to raise your limit again."

"No need, Ed. I actually have a job and will be going back to school soon."

Ed exclaimed, "What? A job. You?"

She smiled smugly. Jason never stopped paying her the harvesting wage because every now and then, she still helped Duke and Danny out. "That's right, I help harvest the apples on my husband's apple orchard."

She knew this was knocking her father over with a feather.

"You've got to be kidding me. What happened to you?"

"Like I told Mallory, I've been reborn. I have a relationship with Christ and I fell in love. I also have a daughter."

He was quiet as he considered what she said.

"Well, good for you then, Lorie."

She felt very emotional after receiving her father's acceptance. That's all she had ever wanted from her parents. Acceptance and love.

"You said you have a daughter? You mean he has a daughter?"

Not wanting to go into it, she simply said, "Yes. And I love her very much. Her name is Abigail."

"Lorelei….for what it's worth, I'm really happy for you."

§

In November, Abby came home for Thanksgiving. They had been texting each other almost every day with a ton of sad faces and I miss you's.

When Jason and Lorelei picked Abby up from the train station, Abby hugged her mom for a full minute.

"Mom, I missed you so much."

"Aww baby, I missed you so much, too."

Jason interrupted, "Can I get any love here, too?" They laughed and had a group hug.

Once they were home, they decided to converge in the coach house to eat and watch *A Charlie Brown Thanksgiving*.

Afterwards, Abby turned off the television and turned towards her parents that were cozied up on the love seat.

"Mom, Dad. I have something to say."

"What is it, baby girl?" Jason asked.

She hesitated and looked down.

"I want to come home."

Jason looked confused. "You are home."

She picked at a fiber on the shag rug beneath her.

"No. I mean I want to come home...for good."

They were quiet as Lorelei's heart stuttered. She didn't say it to Jason too often because she didn't want seem discontent, but she wanted her daughter around so badly. She felt they needed to make up for lost time. She kept quiet and decided to let Jason handle it.

"Why?"

"Because I miss you and mom and I'm so excited about having two parents and I feel like I'm missing out on you guys. I want to go back to Sheridan High."

"What about all of your friends at Whistler?"

"They're cool and all, but not more important than being with you." Close to whining, she said, "Dad, haven't you always told me that family is next under God?"

Impressed with how she turned the tables on him, he answered, "Yes, I have."

"Well, I just found Mom and I want to be with you and her, every day."

He considered what she said and turned to see an anxious Lorelei wringing her hands. Abby looked pleadingly at her.

"Mom, what do you think?"

Lorelei was cautious because she didn't want to go against her husband's wishes. She was still new to this whole wife and mothering thing.

"Well, I'll just be honest. I miss you, too and I would love to be able to see you more often. You know that very well from our texts." Abby grinned. Then Lorelei quickly looked towards Jason. His expression was noncommittal. "But, it depends on what your father thinks."

Abby was now in extreme whine mode. "Dad???"

"If you were to transfer back here, when would that be? You can't just up and leave in the middle of the semester."

"My semester is almost over. Just a few more weeks until Christmas break. Then I can transfer to Sheridan in January. Puhleeaze."

Jason had a twinkle in his eye but continued his stern front.

"Young lady, if this affects your grades in any way, the answer is no. At Christmas, if you've let your grades slip, I'm going to have to refuse."

Abby launched herself into both of their arms from her kneeling position on the floor.

"Oh, thank you Dad! You know I'm a straight A student!"

He knew it and had no doubt that her grades would be impeccable. They always were. Lorelei was learning so much about her new *readymade* family.

§

At Christmastime, sure enough, Abby came home flaunting her six A's. She and Lorelei jumped up in down in delight. Since Thanksgiving, Lorelei had been helping Abby with the documentation necessary to transfer into Sheridan High School.

"Mom, I'm so excited. We don't have to be apart from each other again, that is until I go to college."

"I know, I'm so happy, too. My baby!"

After they finished hugging, they planned to bake Christmas cookies and watch *Santa Claus Is Coming to Town*, an old stop motion animation classic that Lorelei had been watching all of her life. She was thrilled to be able to celebrate a real Christmas with her new family. She had never experienced this before, and Abby, also feeling deprived of a traditional family holiday, reveled in the occasion. They bought decorations, and along with Jason, decorated the tree.

On Christmas Eve, they went to church and gave thanks for the true meaning of the holiday. They held hands Christmas morning as Jason prayed over the big breakfast that Abby had prepared of crescent rolls, omelets, bacon, hash browns and cheesy grits and apple butter made from their very own apples. Everything looked delicious.

"Father God, thank you so much for giving your only begotten Son to be our Savior, Christ. Jesus, we honor you and glorify you on this day in celebration of your birth. Whether this was the actual day you were born or not, it makes no difference. I'm sure you're pleased with all of the love, peace and goodwill that is exchanged on this day. Thank you for your wonderful, amazing gifts this year. Thank you for bringing me my beautiful wife, and thank you for bringing to my daughter, her mother. Thank you for bringing all of us a loving family. In Jesus' Name we pray and give you thanks on your day. Amen."

207

# CHAPTER TWENTY EIGHT

In late May, the three of them were running through the corridors of the hospital.

"Aahhh, Jason!"

He spoke in his authoritative, calm professional voice.

"Calm down, Lorie, you're doing fine. We're here."

In a second, Abby was beside her with a wheelchair, placing her in it and holding her hand that she clenched tightly. She knew she was squeezing the life out of her daughter's hand but she couldn't help it.

"Mom, it's going to be fine.

Lorelei was having contractions that had been coming closer and closer together all morning. She thought about the lady she helped Jason with, Jeanette, and remembered her ordeal in horror.

"Oh no, I don't want to go through what she went through," she wailed.

"Who are you talking about, baby. We're almost to the delivery room."

"Jeanette!"

He smiled. "You remember?"

"Yes, she was in so much pain and her husband wasn't around...Aahhh!"

"I'm right here and you better not call me a fat bastard," he chuckled.

Lorelei half laughed and half wailed.

Abby looked at them in comical confusion.

"We'll tell you later. Just calm your mother down."

Jason had been Lorelei's obstetrician, of course, when they discovered that she was pregnant in January. She had already been four months pregnant and didn't know it, just like with Abby. She had never had regular periods.

Three hours later, Jason was urging her to push. Although she had a C-Section for Abby, she wanted to try a vaginal birth. Jason told her that she wasn't too small to deliver and her pelvis was large enough. In her training sessions with Rose that was now on hiatus, she had been made aware of the many new modern procedures for smaller women if that was their choice.

She was beginning to think she had made a huge mistake.

"Oh MY GOD! I can't do this, Jason. Cut it out of me. Cut it out!" Abby, although nervous as she held Lorelei's hand, began to burst out laughing. Jason, who was down in between Lorelei's legs, was also amused. There was another nurse in the room to assist him.

"Relax, baby. I can see the crown and you're doing fine. You're going to feel a pinch as I do the episiotomy."

"Episiotomy? Oh no! You're cutting my cooch?"

Abby cracked up. "Mom!"

Jason looked up over at Lorelei with humor in his eyes. She was cracking his professional façade with her zaniness.

"Yes, dear. I explained to you that this might have to happen. You're doing just fine."

"She leaned up, sweat gleaming on her face as Abby dabbed her forehead with a wet cloth.

"Well, buster, that means you won't be getting any for a while. Jerk!"

Abby laughed again and the nurse's eyes crinkled behind her mask. She probably thought this family was nuts.

"Mom!" Abby exclaimed. "Calm down. Let Dad do what he has to do."

At her daughter's insistence, she tried to pray and soon after, felt a peace. She definitely wanted Jason to do his job. Thank God she had a sensible daughter and husband. She was sure all of her true crazy colors were on full display.

She felt a pinch and then she was numb down there.

Jason looked up over her legs. "Are you okay, dear? Do you need an epidural? You told me you wouldn't."

Her breath was still ragged but she was calmer.

"I'm fine, but I want to push."

"Not yet, I'll let you know."

"Ooooh," she exclaimed as another contraction hit. She was squeezing Abby's hand hard. She looked up and could see her daughter was nervous for her.

Jason was back down examining her.

"Okay, baby. Ready? One, two, three – Push."

"Uuhhnnnnneeee," she yelled, pushing. Afterwards, she felt as if she couldn't do anymore. She was ready to pass out.

"That was good baby, one more."

"I can't! Noooooo..."

"Come on, baby, one more. The baby's almost here. One more push and I can take the baby out."

"I can't, Jason. I can't. This is too hard," she cried.

She felt wetness and looked up to see that Abby was crying.

She had to get some more strength. She couldn't let her daughter and husband down.

She started to pray out loud. "God, you said I have not because I ask not. Give me the strength, Lord, to bring this life into the world. Aaarggh," she wailed, pushing.

"That's it baby, keep going."

"Eeeeeuuuuhn!"

Then she felt a plop as Jason literally grabbed the life out of her. He suctioned the crying baby's nose and placed the slimy thing on Lorelei's belly. Jason had moisture in his eyes.

"Thank you, baby, you've just given me a healthy son. I've got my boy, now," he said, choking up.

Abby and Lorelei wept as they looked at the baby that had just come into their world. Jason beamed with joy and shed a few tears. She had done it. She had given birth to their beautiful son.

"Wow, Mom. I have a baby brother, now." Abby kissed her and marveled at the infant.

Even now, she could see that he looked like Jason. He had his brown eyes and amazingly, was born with a head full of dark hair. They had purposely avoided knowing the sex and even had Dr. Lillian examine her when it came to ultrasounds. She was mum, of course, to abide by their wishes.

In a string of many lately, this was one of the happiest days of Lorelei's life.

# CHAPTER TWENTY NINE

Later that summer, the four of them landed at O'Hare International Airport.

Lorelei had mixed emotions about coming back to a town that held so much grief, but she knew that she couldn't be afraid. 2 Timothy 1:7 says, *For God has not given us a spirit of fear, but of power and of love and of a sound mind.* She meditated on that all before her flight.

On the plane, she reflected on her activities the last several months while she stayed home to nurse Jason Jr., affectionately called J.J. She was so grateful for her new life and wanted to honor God's wishes. That meant making restitution to as many people as she could regarding her misdeeds. At the time, the best way that she could think of was to send emails apologizing. She still had access to assistants at Sampson Electronics that could get her the contacts she needed. There was one email exchange in particular she fondly remembered…

---

To: Merci Jansen
From: Lorelei Scott
Subject: An Apology
Hello Merci,
I heard you and James were married recently. Sincerely, congratulations. I'm writing you to apologize for my actions when I harmed you and left you in a horrible predicament. I don't know if you can forgive me, but I am truly sorry to

you and James for all of the torment and trouble I caused you. I am a new creature in Christ, now. I have a wonderful husband, daughter and son. As much as you may not believe me, I've changed.

I finally realize how important and precious life is and God has granted me a second chance. I went through a lot, including almost drowning, nodules on my lungs, going to rehab for alcohol dependence, grief with the sex tape I'm sure you're aware of, and a list of other things too long to mention. I'm not forgetting the things I've done, but what I've gone through got me to where I am today. Otherwise, God may not have been able to get my attention. ☺

I'm grateful to have a God that forgives. I know I did awful things, but God has still seen fit to love me, anyway.

I hope you can truly forgive me for putting you in harm's way and I pray you and James have a happy life. I sincerely wish you both the best.

God Bless,

Lorelei Scott *née* Sampson

---

Surprisingly, a day later, she received a reply.

---

To: Lorelei Scott

From: Merci Jansen

Subject: RE: An Apology

Hello Lorelei,

It was a surprise to receive your email. I admit that I didn't want to open it. I wasn't sure what the message would be and in truth, I was expecting vitriol.

However, I was pleasantly surprised to read about the metamorphosis you've gone through. I forgive you. I am also a new creature in Christ along with James. Imagine that! God can do anything, right? ☺

I believe you when you said that you've changed. I know it's possible. It happened to me and to James. With God, all things are possible and He is awesome! Like you, I had to go through some things to get to where I am and I'm also very grateful, so I understand what you're saying.

Let me apologize to you for interfering in a relationship that I should not have. It was wrong and believe me, I paid for it. But with separation, rehabilitation and redemption, God saw fit to bring James and I back together, in the right way.

Congratulations on your new family and I truly wish you the best.

God Bless,

Merci Jansen

---

Grateful for the warm reply and forgiveness, Lorelei felt an immense burden had been lifted and a chapter closed.

§

There was a limo sent to pick them up from the airport. Abby and Lorelei were dressed alike in white capris and alternating glitzy tee shirts while Abby held J.J. They both had their hair down which Lorelei hadn't bothered to color since Abby came into her life. Lorelei was trying to grow it long like her daughter's and they truly looked like sisters.

Jason was on the phone coaching an emergency birth over the phone.

Their first stop was Ed and Mallory's. Afterwards, they planned to sightsee since this was Abby's first visit to Chicago, and then leave tomorrow. She really couldn't think of any reason to stick around after that.

They entered the lobby of her parent's lavish top floor condominium that was much further north up the Gold Coast then hers. Lorelei was amazed at the feelings of distaste she felt for the gaudy atmosphere. She thought she would be forever enamored with this life. Now she could see how empty and sad it had been. Never once fulfilling. She believed there was a hole in each of us that could only be fulfilled by a relationship with Almighty God.

She had only told her mother that she and Jason were coming to town. She made no mention of the other two...guests.

After they climbed the floors on the elevator, she knocked on the door.

"Just a minute," her mother screeched. Lorelei sighed.

Abby and Jason shared a smirk before Mallory wrenched open the door.

She put on her fake welcoming smile, preening and doing the most, of course.

"Wooh, who are all of these people? Wow, Lorelei, he's handsome. Come in, come in."

The four of them entered the residence, Jason and Abby smiling - Lorelei and Little J.J. looking gassy.

Ed was sitting on the sofa looking at them like they had just stepped off the mother ship. Lorelei sighed.

"Mallory, don't tell me you didn't tell Ed we were coming?"

Mallory looked around innocently with a grimace on her face that was supposed to be a smile.

Jason extended his hand to Ed.

"Hello, Sir. Jason Scott."

Bewildered, Ed quickly jumped up and shook Jason's hand vigorously.

"Good to meet you, Jason. I heard about you. You making my little girl happy?"

"I'm trying," he said, laughing. Ed and Mallory looked from them to Abby and Little J.J., now four months, who was squirming. Abby smiled and gave a laugh.

"And who might this gorgeous girl be?" Mallory asked. Then she looked from Abby to Lorelei in puzzlement. "You two look alike. You're dressed alike...your hair..." Mallory and Ed were both looking intently at the two of them.

"That's because she's my daughter, Abigail."

Abby lifted up a hand and waved. "Hi, Grandma and Grandpa."

Mallory gripped her chest and fell backwards towards the sofa while, Ed dutifully caught his wife to calm her down.

"Cut it out, Lorie, you're going to give your mother a heart attack." He tried to think logically. "Now obviously she's Jason's daughter, right?" He looked at Lorelei accusingly. "Lorie, why didn't you tell us that Jason had a daughter...," he looked at Jason, Jr. "who has a child, obviously?"

Lorelei sighed. "Ed, I did tell you Jason had a daughter."

His mind clicked. "That's right. Sorry."

Mallory swatted Ed as she tried to grasp what was happening.

"Why didn't you tell me, ya big dope? Why does the girl have a baby...?"

"Everybody, sit down," Lorelei yelled.

"Oh my goodness, another bombshell. What's everyone going to think when they find out your stepdaughter has a baby. She can't be any older than fifteen."

Abby giggled while Jason tried his best to control his laughter. "I'm sixteen now, Grandma." Abby interjected over all of the chatter.

"Mallory, Ed. Will you just let me talk for goodness sake? Geez!"

"Okay, Lorie, what's really going on?" Ed asked.

"Brace yourself, because I'm not going to keep explaining this. Abby is my daughter. She is my daughter and Jason's daughter."

"I know she's your stepdaughter-"

"No." Lorelei said adamantly. "Let me finish. She is me and Jason's biological daughter."

At this, Mallory started wailing.

"Oh God, what has the tramp done-"

"Hey!" Jason bellowed. "With all due respect, Mrs. Sampson, I told you not to EVER refer to my wife as a tramp again."

Mallory stopped short, shocked at the reprimand. She changed tact and started wailing again. "Oh my God, what has this nut done? What is she talking about? Is she crazy? What's going on?" In disbelief, Jason shook his head.

217

"Calm down, Mal. There's got to be a reason explanation for this. How is Arielle...?"

"Abigail, Grandpa." Abby offered. He blanched but continued.

"Abigail," he enunciated slowly, "how is she both of youse daughter?"

"Please let me explain without any interruption." Lorelei commanded, sighing.

Everyone was finally quiet and she had their attention.

"Okay. Remember the baby I gave up for adoption? She's it. Jason and I went to Liberty High School in Brooklyn together and he's the one who knocked me up sixteen years ago. Get it? Okay. End of story."

Abby and Jason howled with laughter at Lorelei's quick explanation. Abby was delighted to hear her mother's genuine Brooklyn accent that was on ten around her parents.

By this time, Mallory had slid to the floor in despondency with a concerned Ed tending to her.

"Really, Lorie? Is she really the kid?" Ed was always the last to catch on.

"Yes, Ed. And it was only an act of God that brought us all together. That's one of the reasons I believe in Him, now."

"So you two met up and figured all that out. I have to say, that is incredible. Wow." Ed studied Abby and smiled. "Cute kid."

Abby puffed up happily. "Thanks, Grandpa."

Then he looked down at Little Jason that was crying from all of the excitement.

Mallory stopped her antics and glared at Abby. "Now, why did *you* get knocked up? You followed right in your mother's footsteps, I see."

Jason was about to retort when Abby patted her dad's arm, letting him know she had this.

"No ma'am. Although I'm happy Mom gave birth to me when she did - otherwise I wouldn't be here," she laughed, "I don't plan on getting knocked up until I'm married."

Mallory looked at her in confusion.

"Well, whose kid is it?"

"This is our child, Mr. and Mrs. Sampson. This past May, Lorelei gave birth to my son, Jason Derrick Scott, Jr.," Jason announced with pride.

Mallory fainted.

No longer able to hold it in, Jason, Lorelei and Abby burst out laughing. Today had turned out just how they'd thought it would. It was a good thing they all had a sense of humor.

"Mal, Mal, wake up. Mal, wake up." Ed said, fanning his wife.

§

After they all calmed down, they sat down and ate. All throughout dinner, Ed and Mallory were staring at the four of them in amazement. They were trying to adjust to their instant new family members.

Later, her mother called Lorelei off to her bedroom.

"Look, kid. I know I haven't always been...warm or... whatever to you, but...I can see a real change in you." She looked Lorelei up and down, noting the transformation. "You made some different choices. And it's good.

So...okay." She patted Lorelei's hand and turned away uncomfortably.

Lorelei began to cry. That was the most affection she had ever gotten from her mother. She hurriedly wiped her eyes, not wanting her mother to notice. She didn't want to push it.

"Thank you, Mallory."

Abby was watching from the doorway, smiling.

"Mom, I think J.J. is hungry. Should I feed him?"

"You can, sweetheart." She checked her watch to be sure. "It's time."

"Okay." Abby hesitated. "Grandma, will you please let Mom call you Ma? It would really make her happy."

Lorelei shot Abby the eye but couldn't get too mad at her for speaking her mind. She was a chip off the old block. Off two old blocks.

"I tell you what - you're already killing me over here with the whole *Grandma* thing, so...I guess I can live through...that too."

Delighted, Abby smiled. "Thanks Grandma," she said and took off.

Lorelei's heart was bursting with happiness. She knew she had to forgive her parent's for everything they didn't do right. She was ready to move forward. Hence, this visit in the first place.

"Okay, let's try it out. *Mom*," she drew out. There was nothing that could steal her joy.

Mallory flinched but they both laughed.

"Okay, that's enough. Baby steps."

Maybe she had a reason to come back to Chicago, after all...

# EPILOGUE

Lorelei hired a baby sitter, resumed her training with Rose, and took one class in midwifery school that fall per Jason's insistence. With Little J.J., he didn't want her to overdo it.

Having acquired competent top executives to run Sampson Electronics in their absence, Ed and Mallory took an extended vacation for the first time ever. In Savannah.

Lorelei knew it was because they wanted to be around their new grandchildren. She could tell that her parents were beginning to mellow in their golden years.

Jason and Lorelei had been praying for her parents and that their hearts would soften and be open. It didn't happen exactly as they hoped, but there was progress.

Mallory helped by watching J.J. when the babysitter wasn't available or Abby was in school. Ed and Abigail had long talks about various subjects, including their mutual love for baseball. It may not have been an ideal childhood for Lorelei, but the fact that they were trying make some good memories for her children was better late than never.

Who knew?

With God, All Things Really Were Possible.

# ABOUT THE AUTHOR

Traci Morris began writing poetry and stories as soon as she could hold a pencil, her mother attests. Many years in the making, she finally returned to her first love, writing. Traci earned a bachelor's degree in Speech Communications and is also a graphic artist and songwriter. She lives outside of Chicago, Illinois with her family.

## ALSO BY TRACI MORRIS

*Jump Off: The Deep End*